TAILS OF THE ALPUJARRAS

First Published in Great Britain 2015 by Mirador Publishing

First edition: 2015

ISBN: 978-1-910530-80-1

Mirador Publishing
Mirador
Wearne Lane
Langport
Somerset
TA10 9HB

TAILS OF THE ALPUJARRAS
A COLLECTION

FOR THE ANIMALS IN NEED OF SUPPORT IN THE ALPUJARRAS

Contents

Introduction

We are indebted to all the wonderful contributors who have generously donated their work for this anthology. Here is an eclectic mix ranging from bestselling authors to first time writers. The editors have tried to keep editorial interference to a minimum and present the stories with the passion and feel the authors intended. We have a mixture of real life tales and fictional, we have some beautiful and heart-warming stories and we have some which will touch the hardest of hearts. We have poems, anecdotes and heartfelt observations.

By purchasing this you are making a positive contribution to help a lost and desperate animal to survive. All profits are being donated to Valle Verde Rescue. Please share and leave reviews as this raises the profile of the book and will result in more sales and therefore more animals rescued. And if you want to say thank you to the people who have contributed then take a look at some of their other work!

Thank you for buying this copy, you have made a difference.

A Personal Note From The Founders

Valle Verde animal Rescue is a privately run and funded association dedicated to helping abandoned and abused animals from The Alpujarra, Lecrin Valley and Costa Tropical. We set up Valle Verde Animal Rescue after meeting through the wonderful world of Facebook when Linda offered to foster a dog for Freya who had found him in a bad situation and rescued him. The relationship went from strength to strength and we decided to open a Facebook page dedicated to re-homing the many rescue dogs and cats already in Linda's care and the rest is history...

In our short time as an association, just over 12 months, we have homed around 200 animals and we are growing.

Our thanks go out to all of those who have made this book possible, the ideas, efforts and time that have been donated for our cause are as valuable to us as the funding itself.

Thank you all for your ongoing support and the knowledge that together we can build a brighter future for the animals.

Freya and Linda
Valle Verde Animal Rescue

Please visit our website **www.valleverdeanimalrescue.org** and make a change to an animal's life today.

The Near Death Of Bumble from

Last Days Of The Bus Club
By Chris Stewart

Also by this author

The Near Death Of Bumble from

Last Days Of The Bus Club
By Chris Stewart

Picture, if you will, a river raging from its gorge, a truly terrifying tumult of waters, an element gone berserk. As near bonkers as you can get, we, the inhabitants of the far side of that river, had sailed across it suspended from a cable, the 'Flying Fox' as it is known in the trade. Our daughter, Chloé, was going back to Granada.

As we hugged one another goodbye, Bumble, our big white Mastín Leonés, appeared beside us, battered and bedraggled. I could hardly believe that she had launched herself into the raging water and struggled across for no other reason than that we happened briefly to be on the other side. It was little short of a miracle that she had survived. Chloé, delighted by this heroic gesture, smothered her with a big display of affection, while Ana and I tried to disguise our anxiety as to how on earth we'd manage to get the brainless creature home.

Bumble is an enormously strong dog, affectionately known as "The Lifter", for her endearing habit of thrusting her enormous nose deep into the crotch of unsuspecting visitors and, with a heave of her powerful neck, lifting them off the ground. There are some who find this good-natured demonstration of affection embarrassing; we find it a hoot. But there was little lift left in that poor shaken creature shivering and whimpering beside us.

We looked around, appalled at the possibility that Bumble's little terrier companion, Bao, might have tried the same stunt, because he would immediately have been whipped away by the river. But with great relief we spotted him standing anxiously by the cable on the home bank, watching us with that quizzical tilt of the head with which dogs express bafflement.

So Chloé headed off for Granada, and we applied ourselves to the problem of how we were going to persuade Bumble to cross that river again. There was no way we could carry her across on the bo'sun's chair; we're talking about a sixty kilo wriggling mass of dog here. Ana and I swung ourselves across and called to Bumble. But she wasn't having any of it: she took a look at the river, decided against it, and headed downstream.

We followed her, calling and calling. She kept stopping and looking at the river as if assessing where might be a safer spot to cross. And there were better places and worse: in places, you would be battered to death in seconds by the water careering over the rocks, and then there were calmer stretches where you just might stand a chance of swimming across before the current hurled you upon the next heap of rocks. She was clearly still exhausted and terrified by her first crossing, and she continued downstream till the river crashed against a cliff and there was no way past, then turned and headed back up, with us still in pursuit on the other bank.

It's about half a kilometre between the cable and the cliff, and as rough and rocky as you could imagine. There was a spot here that looked good – or at any rate less bad. We stopped and concentrated all we could on trying to persuade the pea-brained animal to come across. We shouted into the noise of the water, and we begged and we cajoled and we jumped up and down with all the energy we could muster, for darkness was falling now and not much time remained. Bumble looked at us piteously, tried the river with a toe, and stepped back. We howled. She stepped in again, a little further this time, and was instantly knocked off her feet, disappearing beneath the water as she roiled away down the river only to be smacked hard against a rock. Somehow she righted herself and staggered out of the water on the same side as she had entered.

'Let's try walking away,' suggested Ana. 'She might pluck up courage if she sees us going home.' So we did, looking back over our shoulders and calling out as we clambered across the rocks. The pitiful creature gazed at us imploringly as we abandoned her, then hurled herself one more time into the water. We raced back to the bank and howled encouragement. Again she vanished beneath the water, hurled downstream by its awful force. We were quiet for a moment ... and then we saw her again, scrabbling with her claws to haul herself onto a flattish rock in the middle of the river. She slipped and half fell, but her desperation saved her and she heaved herself up and lay limp and exhausted on the rock.

The dog was not more than a dozen metres from us now. We watched her in the dying light, panting in a state of dazed terror, letting her rest a little to recover some strength. And then we yelled together and yelled and yelled at her to throw herself in just one more time and give it all she'd got and she'd be here. She struggled to her feet and moved to the edge of the rock ... but on the wrong side; she seemed about to head back where she had come from. Ana and I nearly went berserk, screaming our very lungs out. If she got this wrong she would be done for. The river on the far side of the rock was wider and nastier; she had already done the harder bit ... and now it looked like she was going back. 'BUUMMMBBLE, YOU BRAINLESS BERK! HEEEEERE, OVER HERE!'

She sniffed the water, stumbled, and unsteadily shuffled round to look at us, frantic with fear. Ana was almost in tears by now and I was beside myself. And then the wretched dog threw herself into the water towards us. She vanished instantly, dragged under by the current. That awful infinitesimal moment seemed to stretch on and on as we waited to see her head above the water again, but we could see nothing.

We stumbled downriver over the boulders, peering desperately into the gathering gloom and the tumult for some sight of her, but there was nothing, and we couldn't risk getting any closer to those terrible waters. But still we yelled Bumble's name, as if resisting the thought that we had had our last sight of her.

And then, after twenty or so minutes of this, we stopped. It was dark now. We could barely see the boulders in front of us. We had to accept that she had gone. Another dog down. That's how it is with dogs: they die on you. You have to get over it, and she had had a good innings. I was deeply upset, though. Bumble may have been something of a bimbo but she was affectionate and dependable. Wherever I went, she'd be with me, thumping that enormous tail of hers, making us laugh with her nonsensical notions and habits. Ay, Bumble ... taken by the river.

I put my arm round Ana's shoulders and we stood there in silence, enveloped by the roaring of the river, as a few more minutes passed. And then, as if by some unspoken agreement, we turned and started to pick our way back towards the house. By the big Eucalyptus tree we stopped and looked back once more towards the river in the dark.

'Well,' I said, 'at least it was quick. I guess it's not a bad way to go. And she never got incontinent, like old dogs do ...' Ana was silent. I warmed to my theme. 'She's a big dog. You don't want a dog that big being incontinent about the place, do you?'

I had thought I might try and make Ana laugh – although the conceit was not a particularly funny one, and it was hardly a time for levity. A respectable period ought to elapse before one dwelt upon the humorous aspect of a dog's death. And then I laughed. I laughed and laughed. Because there, pale and sodden in the darkness, was the great bedraggled berk of a dog, panting and feebly attempting to wag her tail. We threw ourselves upon her. One hell of a dog, that one.

A Guilty Tail

By David Bull

A Guilty Tail

By David Bull

So I'm on the phone to an important customer when my black Labrador, Woopy, piles into the office chasing her tail which is all fine and dandy if, 1. You are aware of the furniture and people around you and, 2. If you haven't chased it (and not caught it) at least 15,000 times before – like yesterday. But Woopy is nothing if not persistent and ignorant of any appeal to stop until boredom or a walk is looming.

The idea, the same idea s she's had since day one, is to take her tail by surprise; by somehow leaping at speed towards where he tail was a split second before. She has convinced herself that this method is possibly going to prove more fruitful than the standard running-around-in-circles-for-ages technique.

The noise of dog on table and then table on floor has me putting my finger in my ear as my, by now, laughing client (thank goodness for that) listens to the racket. Things quietened down a little when she gradually mummified herself in the curtains until the pole threatened to come down, which it did. Woopy made the customary 'leggit' move while I finished my call and tidied up only to find her leaning against the open fridge chewing chicken tikka and wagging a guilty tail…

Alegria

By Meg Robinson

I came to Las Apujarras for a week in 1996, 19 years ago, and am still here! Like so many people, I got zapped by the beauty and the specialness of this part of the world. Between '96 - 2002 I divided my time between Las Alpujarras in the winter, and Alaska in the summer. I continued to be nomadic for 5 years, then bought a little house here and renovated it. Since then I have published a travel memoir, www.drawnbyastar.com -Adventures in Patagonia, and 6 books of my paintings and photographs with www.blurb.com. I've become a fundraiser for 5 projects for disadvantaged children in Bolivia and Peru. Although not a dog owner, I am very happy to support Valle Verde.
http://www.drawnbyastar.com/

Alegria

By Meg Robinson

Friday 13th is frequently said to be an unlucky day, but for me last year, it brought pure happiness on four little legs.

My day started early. I was in Motril, in Andalucía, by 9am. The garage opened at 8.30.

The fine grey material covering the inside of the roof of my 18 year old car had come unstuck in places, so driving had become hazardous. It was like having a small parachute vigorously bouncing up and down off my head all the time, much worse when the window was open. There was a real possibility of becoming en-shrouded at any moment, so, it had to be fixed.

The repair job was going to take four hours, and it would cost 100€.

It was early July. Baking hot. Motril is beside the sea. On a clear day, from the port, you can see the Riff Mountains of Morocco. Today a heat haze glazed the horizon.

I took a new book to read to bide my time. However temping, it was far too hot to explore the city, or the port, or the Chinese Emporium.

The book had been waiting for me in the Post Office for at least three weeks. It's hard to park in that part of town. If you have any mobility challenges like a seriously dodgy hip, as I have, walking any distance is challenging. I was delighted to finally collect my new paperback. Perfect timing I thought. Called 'An Irish Tale of a Modern Mystic' the author, Tantra Matt, was a friend of a friend.

Ireland is my homeland, Spain is where I've lived for the last 18 years.

The day promised to be a scorcher. To pass the four hours comfortably, I planned to move from cafe to cafe, reading, alternating between decaf coffees and glasses of ice cold water.

9am.

While enjoying my first delicious café con leche on the terrace of the bar opposite the garage, my attention was taken by a filthy little dog, shaking with fear. Completely confused, he seemed to be searching for his owner, or desperately trying to come up with a plan B. Where to go, what to do next?

Obviously abandoned, he was a picture of horrible neglect. His mangy long tail looked like a feather duster dipped in sick.

I tried to attract his attention. This is not a habit of mine, I assure you. I am not a doggy person, yet. He smelt the food from the bar and came closer. Then he noticed me making odd faces and strange noises, and smiled, well, something akin. It didn't take long for us both to fall deeply in love.

And when it happened, he transformed into a joyful little acrobat, dancing around me, leaping half cartwheels in the air, licking my bare toes, shivering with delight. Every few seconds he stopped to scratch. Finally he came to rest lying on my feet, *tranquillo*, safe, snug, and peaceful.

My heart was kidnapped.

I called him *Alegria* (Happiness*), Pura Alegria.*

His transformation was awesome.

With the smallest bit of effort on my part, laced with loving encouragement and the intention to calm his fear, the bright happy clown in him popped out, and I told him that if he was here when I came back for my car, I'd take him home and love him.

Next cafe. 10am.

Tantra's book was drawing me deeply into realms of the mysterious. Being Irish, it was all strangely familiar. Ireland is my homeland, Spain is where my heart is happy.

The noise of the traffic vanished as I read about wild Ireland, my birth country, my lost heritage, the place of my primal wound. The country where, as a baby, my little life had been like *Alegria's*, well kind of… disowned, abandoned, but then adopted.

Excitedly I recognised a few of the characters and places mentioned in the book. Highlighting lines I wanted to remember, I was intrigued by the authors extraordinary psychic gifts and courage.

Next café. 11am.

40 degrees at least. More ice cold drinks needed.

Sipping from a tall slim glass of deliciously chilled grape juice, I felt inexplicably linked to a mysterious flow of pure *alegria.*

Why had this filthy little dog opened the door of my heart so wide?

'The power of a mystery is that you can never fully understand it. You only experience it. This is the joy of heaven on earth. I let myself be held by this energy,'' writes Tantra Matt.

I certainly let myself be held by that energy of Love all morning, and many surprising things started to happen every time I moved cafe!

Each time I looked up from reading, I saw right in front of me a person with an extremely severe leg problem. Each leg problem was different. I watched how these brave people managed to move with their sticks or crutches, how they sat down, how they got up. I noticed how fiercely independent they all wanted to be. Even in 40 degrees, they were not deterred by disability.

20

Tantra Matt, whose book I now couldn't put down, brings Americans of Irish origin back to their roots on Vision Quests, so they can 'remember who there were, and what they've forgotten.'

She writes:

'I realize that we all long to be recognized for who we truly are. Why ? Without being seen as what we truly are, something fundamental is missing. We are run by fear. When we know who we are, we trust our choices. Risk is easier because what we are risking is based on the strength and clarity that comes from that deep self-knowledge.'

12 noon.

I trusted my choice to adopt *Alegria* - if he was still at the cafe.

He wasn't.

Postscript.

I believe *Alegria* found in any form is never really lost. I think it makes its way straight into the tenderest part of the heart, which is a kind of welcome room, waiting for new arrivals.

I also believe friendship is an 'Act of Devine Recognition' even with or maybe especially with animals. I hope this little creature, where ever he is now, has a loving home.

He has certainly found a home in my heart, forever.

Before Friday 13th 2014, I didn't know about Dog Love. I didn't know personally a dog could touch your heart so much you would want to take it home and care for it.

Many friends are besotted by their dogs, this has always been a fathomless mystery to me.

Por fin (at last) I understand why.

I've joined the club guys, count me in!

And Sit

By Charlotte Moore

www.charlotte-moore.com

And Sit

By Charlotte Moore

"And SIT!"

Humums and Hudads stopped in unison as the bundle of legs on the end of the lead took not a bit of notice and carried on sniffing around. Sophie the Springer wagged her tail and the minute her owner looked down at her she promptly rolled on her back and proffered her tummy up for a rub. Casper, so called as he was all white but of what breed was not really determinable, did actually sit; but then promptly nipped at his owners trouser leg. Joey the cocker-sheltie cross sniffed at his owners leg, cocked and weed. With a startled yelp from his owner, he sat, looked up with innocent eyes and gave a tiny bark that was more like a mew and wagged his tail. Thankfully the trainers had wet wipes and towels to mop up the puddle. Joey thought it amusing that the next group after puppy training was aerobics and they would be prancing around his puddle.

"And again ladies and gents. This time try to be a bit more assertive in your tone when you say 'sit,' Rover is not going to learn unless you teach him. Walk on." The raggedy walk began once more around the village hall. "Remember to keep your voices high and happy when you give instructions." A high pitched chorus of 'heel Jenny', 'come Toby' could be heard over the plaintive puppy woofs as the untrained crew progressed in a clockwise fashion, "And SIT." Sophie rolled over and wagged, Casper sat, and Joey? Joey looked around and spied a Great Dane who had arrived late and promptly tried to tug his unsuspecting owner across the room. The trainer quickly tugged at his lead. "Naughty girl, stop that!"

"He's a boy," said his humum.

"Ah yes, sorry. You mustn't let him tug like that, he could pull you over."

She took the lead off hu-mum, "now sit, Joey." She gave a swift upward movement with her arm and Joey caught the smell of treats. Now Joey liked treats. He sat. "Good boy Joey, good boy." She patted Joey on the head and gave him his reward, a dog biscuit. Joey sniffed at the offering in her hand. He didn't like biscuits. Biscuits were not for him, he liked meat. He looked up at the trainer and stood up. "Oh, meaty treats for Joey then, try to work on that. Sausages. A pocket of sausages is always good." She turned her back and went back to the centre of the room. Joey and humum edged their way back in line, humum feeling chastised, Joey wanting sausage now it had been mentioned and all the time he was still glaring at the Great Dane. Long legs and lolling ears, he would be fun to play with.

"Right, one last time before we have a demonstration of what you will learn next week, walk on."

The dozen or so puppies were tiring after an hour of organised dragging so quite obediently and without much argument, they all walked and wobbled their way around the room one last time. "And sit." To a one, they all sat, happily munched on yet another treat then most lay down hoping for a snooze. With a belly full of treats and not knowing whether to sit, stand, walk, heel or pee they were exhausted. Kiera the Podenco jumped up into her owner's arms, snuggled under his neck and promptly fell asleep: oblivious of all the oohs and ahs from all present and the embarrassment of her owner, a bearded and tattooed Hells Angel in full leather garb. Kiera was a special rescue as she had come all the way from Spain. Tony her hudad had been biking over in Andalucia with his friends when they had come across a rescue centre for strays called Valle Verde Animal Rescue when they had stopped one evening for a beer and got chatting to some friendly locals at the next table. Over the next hour or so they decided to visit and see for themselves and the expected happened, Tony and his friend Joe fell for a couple of podencos and on their return to the UK had arranged to adopt them. It was an anxious wait as they were vetted and the dogs passports acquired. Transport was arranged and then Kiera and Boss were in the UK and into the arms of their waiting new homes.

"Right everyone, your attention for a few more minutes as Harvey shows you how to walk to heel properly, sit, walk on, turn, sit and lie down to command." Joey's attention was once again centred on Harvey. It was the Great Dane that came late and lolled on the stage watching them all with a superior air. Joey yanked on his lead and almost succeeded in breaking free

24

but humum pulled him back. He settled in humum's lap as she had sat down to watch. 'Wasn't this where I peed earlier?' thought Joey. "Ok Harvey, let's see how it's done."

Harvey's hudad Peter was a lovely old bloke who had sat in a chair all evening, almost nodding off until the tea and biscuits had been produced. He had promptly come to life and nabbed the last 2 Bourbons on the plate. Harvey hadn't even looked up at him with pleading eyes, he had just stayed watching all the puppies. Peter had nibbled away at the biscuits, dunking in his tea occasionally and was left totally oblivious of the crumb trail down his chest until he stood up to give the demonstration. A swift brush down made the nearest dog, which happened to be Sophie the Springer, spring into action and vacuum up the crumbs in super quick time. With a lick of the lips she lay back down awaiting a belly rub from humum for being such a good girl. Humum blushed and didn't know whether to praise or ignore. Peter popped on Harvey's lead and in an almost inaudible voice called him to heel. Harvey came to his left side and sat, no lolling to one side, he sat perfectly straight and looked up at Peter. "Walk on Harvey." Harvey stood and walked calmly at Peter's side, his eyes flicking up to Peter all the time as they progressed around the room. Peter gave the command 'close in' and as a one they turned to face the other way and continued walking back in the direction they had come. "And Sit," again barely audible. Harvey sat, Peter pointed at the ground and Harvey lay down. Peter let go of his lead and walked away. Harvey stayed put. A spontaneous round of applause from around the room and a lot of worried looks from humums and hudads wondering if their little darling would ever be able to do that. Joey was once more glaring at Harvey as he was called by Peter and walked back past the other dogs.

A few weeks later and the hall was once more full of bright and eager faces and boisterous puppies. Any learnt discipline went out of the window as they each entered the room, it was like old friends meeting. Tails wagged and owners were dragged across the room as dogs greeted one another and once one dog found their voice it was a chain reaction of barking: the evening chorus. Treats were being passed around from one owner. She had chewy sausage ones and biscuit ones in different pockets, something for every one of them. Looking around the Bichon Frise twins had not turned up. Both were always dressed immaculately in matching blue diamante collar and lead and pink diamante collar and lead [you have to wonder at owners sometimes]. They were an odd pair, one very outgoing, Todd and the other very timid,

Lucy. Lucy hated to be away from Todd but also didn't seem to want to walk! They had come with both huparents but whilst Todd would happily parade around, Lucy would refuse to walk at all and slid along the floor like a mop before stumbling to her feet for a few paces and then flopping back down again. Even when one of the trainers gave them extra attention it made no difference, Lucy just didn't like being amongst all the other dogs.

Harvey was already in his place on the stage but tonight he was sitting next to a black standard poodle. She was flirting with him furiously with little yelps and nibbles at his ear. You could see she was trying to contain herself but her little pompom tail was beating the stage floor like a drum of doggy love. Her owner was trying to pull her away but she was having none of it, she liked Harvey and she was going to get her man. As Harvey had long since had the necessary paraphernalia to have little PooDanes removed, it was of no worry to the owners. Joey's humum was chatting to Sophie's humum. Sophie like Joey was a rescue pup. She and her siblings had been abandoned in a park and Joey's previous owner had died and he had been placed in kennels by the family. Technically Joey wasn't a pup as he was 10 but he acted like one and needed training so humum had brought him along in hope of some discipline. He was a funny little fella really. He absolutely adored people but had no idea what to do around other dogs. His heart raced and although he looked eager to join in and his tail was wagging, if another dog was too friendly too quickly he would bark at them. But he did like Sophie and a little Yorkshire Terrier called Tez.

A clap of the hands and the chatting stopped, "into your circle please and when you are ready, walk on."

Off they were dragged until they got the feel of things. "And sit." They all sat. "Walk on." They all walked on, "close by then walk on" they all turned and walked perfectly. Sophie still insisted that once she had sat for a nanosecond, she could lie on her back for a belly rub. This did on occasion, now that most of the dogs were pals end up with a rather excited boy dog or two exploring further than they really should have in the light of a village hall! Little Tez didn't really care much, he did as he was told and did that thing that tiny Yorkies do: he stood and dithered. Casper as from day one, was the consummate professional and did everything his owner told him to do. Joey by now had learnt that he could get fed if he did as he was told. Over the previous weeks he had flustered his poor owner and nipped at her as she had tried to firmly lower his back end into a sit and stood stubbornly when he

26

was encouraged to lie down. Then Peter had introduced the treat idea. In effect, bribery and the world began to look rosier. It took three attempts to get Joey to sit for a treat and just two to get him to lie down. He had even progressed swiftly onto 'leave it' when a treat was placed in front of him. The only thing was that now whenever he got in after a walk he sat for a treat and at bedtime he waited for a 'leave it' treat too. He had his humum sussed good and proper.

Today was a big test. It was 'sit, stay and walk away' day: letting go day. Owners were quiet after what was now the warm up walk around, they had to let their fur babies go. Would they behave?

Off the stage lolloped Harvey as Peter brought him into the centre. "What Peter will do is keep Harvey calm with a little walk around and then get him to sit, stay, remove his lead and walk backwards about six foot then walk back to him, attach his lead and praise and reward him." As she was stalking Peter was doing his settling walk with Harvey. Harvey was more interested in the jacket that lay on the floor. The Hells Angel had cast it aside when he got warm. Harvey could smell treats so wanted to divert to the jacket, much to the horror of Peter who was having to drag his nose out of the pocket! Order restored by the trainer dragging the jacket to the other end of the hall, [she was a slight five foot tall and the jacket weighed more than she did] Harvey did another circuit before being ordered to sit. The hall was quiet, all eyes on Harvey for his big moment. Peter whispered for him to sit and stay, removed his lead then stepped backwards. Harvey stayed perfectly still, his eyes on Peter. Peter walked back and reattached the lead, gave him a treat and walked the hall to applause. It was obvious Peter enjoyed it as much as Harvey.

"Let's all line up down the room so we can learn the step away before we each take turns doing this. It should be easy if you've been practicing it." Nervous glances all around as everyone got in place to practice bottoms stuck out in mid air as their huparents distanced themselves as far as possible from their pets whilst still holding their leads. The dogs were just waiting for a treat. "Casper, you first please." Casper's hudad led him happily to the top of the room as everyone else went quiet. Good as gold, Casper settled: sat, stayed and was duly rewarded. Things were off to a good start. Sophie's turn. Her owner was quite flushed as she took the walk up the hall. Those that had done it were smiling and murmuring encouragement, the rest were quietly trying to blend in with the walls. For once Sophie sat and didn't roll over for once for a fuss. For once she sat bolt upright all eyes on her humum. Humum unclipped her lead and started the walk backwards. Sophie stayed put. You could see the delight on humums face that this little bundle of energy was actually doing what she was being asked. You could see the tension drain out of humum's shoulders as she relaxed and started the walk back to Sophie, already celebrating in her head that Sophie hadn't shown her up. She attached her lead and gave her a big fuss along with a couple of treats and to a ripple of applause started to walk back down the hall. Which was when the laughter changed to a gasp and Sophie's lead went taught. Humum turned her head to witness Sophie stoop and do her business in the middle of the hall.

Buddy – Perro Español

By Jane Walters

Jane Walters has her head in England, but her heart in Spain and often writes amusing 'stuff' on her blog at www.hellosixty.com

Buddy – Perro Español

By Jane Walters

Oh here comes another human for a bit of a look round, and she's blonde, that makes a change.

No point in getting my hopes up, she's on her own. No hombre. She'll definitely be wanting a pequeño perro, that's for sure; one that fits nicely under her arm, and, more importantly into her life.

Nope, she won't be interested in a big, black, hairy no good mutt like me.

ENTRANCE TO THE DOG SHELTER

It was the beginning of May when, with time on my hands I rocked up at the local dog shelter in Spain and found myself standing outside a HUGE compound, where around 100 small dogs were heading towards me, full of untapped energy, all clearly wanting some attention.

But I wasn't there to adopt a dog.

I was just intending to lend a hand wherever I could. I'd just spend an hour or two there, pat a few heads, throw the odd ball, and maybe brush a few teeny tiny dogs to make them more presentable and help them find that forever home.

Or so I thought.

I was expecting to find around 50 dogs at the dog shelter, so nothing could have prepared me for the 300 that were actually there, not to mention another 100 or so cats. As for the patting of heads and throwing of balls, no chance, there was far more important work to be done.

For goodness sake pipe down you noisy lot. It's just the Senora with her mop and bucket, she's got 4 kennels to muck out before she gets to us.

Looks like I was mistaken too, the blonde one is scraping and sweeping, maybe she's here to help rather than rehome.

I'll see how she is before I get too friendly. Volunteers don't usually last long. She'll be here for one day, gone the next.

I soon got the hang of it. 10 kennels to a block to be scraped, swept, hosed and disinfected one at a time. 5 dogs to be counted out of each kennel, water and food bowls to be topped up, and 5 dogs to be counted back in again. All under clear blue skies and searing heat.

I'd never shovelled so much shit in all my life!

But what a strange sense of achievement as each initially stinky, poo infested kennel, was restored to order, and smelling much more appealing due to a generous sloshing of dog friendly disinfectant.

Yes of course I did throw a few balls, I patted plenty of heads and gave as many dogs as I could some individual attention.

It soon became clear that the mantra of any dog shelter volunteer has to be that you can't save them all. But you can help to keep the environment clean, and the animals safe and healthy, so that when a potential forever family does show up, each dog has the best possible chance of getting a new home.

Thank goodness it's our turn. She's been ages getting to us, and a bit slow with the sweeping. I'll go and have a sniff at her, see if I get any reaction. Probably not. I could do with a haircut, I'm not looking my best.

I've been here a while, and I know it's much easier to bath the little 'uns. I'm one of the biggest in here, and the least likely to attract attention. I wish I was small, and white and fluffy and cute, but the truth is, I'm big and black, and hairy, and as I've already been here over a year, I know my days are numbered now.

Hang on a minute, I can smell something interesting.

Praise the doggy Lord, I think its cheese! CHEESE, we never get cheese, and in tiny cubes too, this is such a treat. I like this woman, I'll just hang around her, see if she has any more cheese up her sleeve.

As each kennel door was opened, it was utter chaos. 5 dogs with lots of pent up energy eager to get out for the 15 minute window of running opportunity. I got to the last kennel in the block and 4 dogs were almost hanging off the wire mesh of the door, waiting to make their escape, whilst dog number 5, a big black hairy mutt just ambled over and sniffed me.

BLACK DOG IN HIS KENNEL

I'd got no pockets in my shorts, so had shoved some cubes of cheese up my sleeve in small plastic bag. All of the other dogs had missed the treats, but not this one. He never left my side while I cleaned out his kennel and he ate ALL my cheese!

Finally after 4 hours of continuous hard slog, the job was done, all the kennels were clean and it was time to leave. I said my goodbyes to all the dogs, with a special pat on the head for the cheese loving perro, and promising that I'd be back in a couple of days, I drove away.

I know, I know, I should have shared the cheese, but it's not often I get a look in, and so yep, it was me. I ate all the cheese.

I think we are out of dog food, so l hope we get our usual delivery of stale bread this afternoon, so at least we get something for supper.

Everyone does their best, but sometimes funds run out and so we always need kind people to donate a few euros.

That blonde one was alright. She actually made a fuss of ME. Nobody ever does that. I hope she comes back. Preferably with cheese.

BREAD DELIVERY

I did go back. For the next six weeks, I swept and shovelled, twice a week, and it simply got hotter and hotter. The dogs began to get used to me, and now my treat bag bulged with goodies mainly for the 'black dog'.

Out of all the dogs I came across, he was by far the most laid back. He calmly draped himself over the pitched roofs of two beaten up old dog kennels and simply 'dog watched' most of the time. He was regarded as one of the cleanest, friendliest residents. He was well mannered and sociable with his kennel mates, and I knew I was singling him out for special attention and looked forward to seeing him.

Here she comes, even above the flippin din this lot make I'd know the sound of her car anywhere, and she always calls out 'Hola Perro' in a sing songy kind of way as she's working.

It's getting SO hot now, she's throwing more water over herself than she's putting in the buckets. I hope she doesn't just disappear like the others do. She's the first one who has ever paid me any attention. Imagine, just imagine if by some miracle, one day, she decided to take me home with her.

But no. There is still no hombre. She probably has a tiny piso, with no room for an ungainly great mutt like me. Dream on.

Soon the end of June arrived, and on what was just about the hottest day I had ever encountered at the dog shelter, I sadly knew that I couldn't continue to work in the blazing sunshine, shovelling piles of poo for one more day. Maybe I was a lightweight, but, as a fair skinned, blonde woman, of a certain age and I knew there were other ways I could help the dog shelter.

I walked up and down the rows of kennels for one last time, took pictures

33

and silently wished that I could simply take them all home and give them a good life. But that was impossible.

I got to kennel number 5 to say a last 'Goodbye' to my favourite perro, and give him one last treat.

He ambled off his lookout point, and came across to the door of the kennel, and for some reason, as I bent down to stroke his head he licked the side of my face, something he'd never done before.

We had a bit of a chat, as you do, and I told him to be a good boy, and walked away feeling more than a bit sad.

I'm not sure what she's up to. The cleaning is all done, and she's taken a few pictures with her camera. She's got a bit of a sad face on, and she's stopping at each kennel and talking to a few of my doggy mates. She was a bit slow with the sweeping today, and there was a lot of huffing and puffing going on although to be fair, most of us dogs were at it too.

Hang on, here she comes. I'll go over, see what occurring. Blimey, she does look sad, I'd better give her a kiss, maybe that'll make her feel better. Mmmm bit salty, but I gave it my best shot.

She's talking in a different way, and I'm not sure I like it much. It sounds to me as if this is 'Goodbye'. I've just got that feeling. Dogs have a sixth sense you know, and we are not often wrong.

I think she's walking away. For good.

Only I didn't walk away.

As I passed the 'office' to go back to my car, something made me go in, and tell them that I wanted to take the black dog home.

We found the oldest of collars, and took a lead back to the kennel number 5, then took him through the mayhem of the other 100 small dogs that were all running lose, to the exit of the shelter.

Humans, honestly they'd forget their head if it wasn't stuck on. She must have forgotten something. Is it her bag, or her sunglasses?

What's that in her hand, a collar and lead, oh goodie, looks like she decided to take me for a quick walk before she goes home.

There, very unceremoniously, he was tied to the bumper of my car, microchipped and vaccinated in seconds. I handed over 100 euros, and in return, the paperwork, passport and dog were handed over to me.

OUCH, no really OUCH! Some walk that turned out to be. She just took me out into the car park and then someone stuck a big needle in my neck and punctured me with what looked like a gun.

34

I'm up for complaining about this rough treatment.

I know I quite like her, but now she's taking a liberty with me. OUCH! What? So now you expect me to jump in the boot of your car do you?

Well, I have no idea why, but I'll do anything to get away from this lot and their needles.

I lifted the boot of my estate car, he jumped in, and with the warm breeze blowing through his flappy ears and scruffy coat, we drove away, and didn't look back.

BUDDY 4 YEARS LATER

The 'black dog' was renamed 'Buddy', and my impulsive decision has turned out to be one of the best I've ever made.

From the minute I drove him away from the shelter, he has honestly been the perfect dog. We lead quite a nomadic existence, sometimes in the UK, sometimes in Spain, but he simply knows that if he can see me, he's safe and wherever we lay our collective hats, then that is 'our' home, for however long.

Initially, he was scared of the outside world, men in hats, children playing on bikes and traffic in general. But gradually, he has gained confidence and now it's just the odd hot air balloon which sends him running for cover.

For the first week or so, he slept and slept. It was almost as if he had at last found some peace and quiet, away from the noise of hundreds of other dogs, and he was distressing himself.

He took some time to understand that any bowl of food was ALL his, and he didn't have to keep running up, grabbing a bit, and gulping it down as fast as possible in case another dog stole it.

He is a gentle, happy, quiet boy, who never needs to be told off, or chastised in any way. He has slotted into my life so easily, it's as if we were made for each other.

Of course not everyone can rehome a dog but even if you just have a few hours to spare now and again, do get in touch with your local dog shelter and offer your help. They will be so grateful.

Or if you don't have time on your hands, but could spare even as little as 5 euros a month, ANY dog shelter would be just as grateful for your support.

She's MINE, all mine. She belongs to ME, she's MY MUMMY!

I've looked after her for 4 years now, and as long as she can see me, she's knows safe.

Phew, at first it was scary I can tell you, all the cars, noisy kids, men with strange things on their heads, even now I'm not keen on things that drift over our house breathing fire.

But gone are the days when I had to fight over a washing up bowl full of food with 4 other dogs, and when I couldn't hear myself think for the barking and arguments that sometimes raged in the kennel.

I won't lie to you, I should have been called 'Lucky'. I get taken out for two long walks a day, I can sleep wherever I want, and even get taken to the hairdressers for a wash and blow dry.

I've got a new group of friends, I see in the park every morning when we hang out and play ball, and a virtual army of people begging to look after me if my Mum ever has to nip off somewhere.

But if she does have to go off for an hour or two and buy new shoes or treats for me, I just snooze, and wait, I know she will always come home. And when she does, I always let her know I'm happy to see her. Sometimes I even get a bit confused and think that she's been gone for hours, when in fact she's just been hanging the washing out. Funny that.

We live a quiet life, me and my Mum. I watch her every move while she taps away at her computer, waiting for the 'walkies' signal. I follow her around everywhere, so I don't miss anything, although she draws the line when she goes in the smallest room of the house. I have to wait outside the door.

Of course, when I'm quiet she thinks I'm asleep, but I'm not. After all, she rescued me from a fate that probably was death, so I will love her and look after her forever.

I'm a dog, and that's just what we do.

JANE WALTERS and BUDDY
Find Buddy on Facebook at *BUDDY-El-Perro-Espanol*

Saxon

By David Luddington

Also by this author

The Return Of The Hippy
The Money That Never Was
Schrodinger's Cottage
Forever England

Saxon

By David Luddington

I did my best 'Good Boy' face and nudged at the leg of the man who had the food. It was a warm day again and the plaza was full of people. I like warm days, people eat food outside on warm days and the place where all the tables and chairs are is the best hunting. The only problem was that warm days also brought much competition and the big black mongrel, Snarler I think he calls himself, likes to control the area. He doesn't scare me though, I'm still small and fast and he's slow. Too many fights have left their mark on his body.

The man ignored my nudge and continued to talk to his lady across the table from him. I weaved between his legs and then headed to the other side of the table to try my luck with her. Unlike many of the ladies here, her legs were covered the same as the man's. That was a shame, I like lady's legs, they feel soft. I sat and stared upwards. Recently, I'd learned that drooping my ears and staring can improve my chances. I drooped and stared. Although her talking noises didn't stop and her gaze never shifted from her man, her hand dropped low towards me. It held a piece of meat. I nibbled it from her hand then licked her fingers clean for her. I caught a taste of something faintly familiar, not from the meat but from the lady herself. I licked round the back of her hand to try to catch it. I couldn't quite recall what it was. She idly stroked my head then pushed me away. That was confusing. I sat and stared again. Nothing. I padded my front feet up and down in a sort of imitation walking movement. I've learned that often gets attention. Her hand came down again. More meat? No, it was an unfriendly hand this time and it pushed at me until I moved away.

Humans are very confusing creatures. They seem to want us around but then they send us away. Sometimes they act like real pack leaders and guide us to shelter and food and other times they beat us. I don't understand.

I headed for a different table. This one already had a dog in attendance but that was Bin Diver, he was okay and he didn't mind sharing his table and besides, there were lots of humans at this one, a real pack. I found my target, a human with long hair on his head and his face. I stared. It wasn't long before I was rewarded. He looked at me and made warm talking noises. His eyes said he was pleased to see me and I wagged my tail to reciprocate. He bent over towards me and broke some food into bits. He gave me the biggest of them. A true pack leader. I gulped it down and when I looked up at him he gave me his piece as well. Bin Diver came and sat next to me, clearly also recognising this particular human as a good alpha. The man continued to feed us both and soon we had eaten enough to quiet the hunger. However we stayed until he stopped feeding us as it's never good to turn food away even if one's stomach is already full.

When the man stopped sharing his pack food with us I jumped up to try to clean him but I'm still new and small so I could only reach halfway up his covered leg. Feeling satisfied, I headed off to the small tree area and settled into the warm dirt and went to sleep.

***

I awoke when the sun was fading and I started to feel the cold. I went over to where the nice human had been but there was nobody at the tables now, only a few of the noisy humans who gather in the corner. They were selfish and never any good for food. I saw Hunter across the other side of the Plaza, he's a big dog and great fun to play with. He was chasing one of those round, brightly coloured things that usually collect under the trees. I ran over to him and tried to take it from him. He growled at me in his pretend fierce way then jumped on me. We rolled around on the ground with me trying to nip his legs with my sharp, young teeth while he tried to use his size to squash me. This was always fun but very tiring. Hunter is big and heavy but he is also a very skilled fighter and he has taught me much. He sometimes lets me win, which is nice.

After we had played for a while I felt the pain of the hunger return and went in search of humans. A man sat on a bench drinking from a big bottle. He had food in a bag by his side, I could smell it. I sat in front of him and stared. He looked down at me and growled loud human noises. His foot swung out and although I saw it coming I wasn't fast enough to avoid it. The booted foot thumped into my side and threw me some distance across the ground. The man stood and made more growling noises, coming towards me once more. I managed to get to my feet and get away from him just before the boot came again. Despite the pain I was able to run into the small tree place and hide.

When the dark came I thought it might be safe to come out again. A group of noisy humans were at one of the tables in the plaza. They had lots of bottles on the table, that usually means they are feeding so they might share. I chose a man and did my good boy face. He noticed me straight away and held some food out for me. I had to stretch up for it as it was just out of my reach but the food moved away. The human couldn't see I was unable to reach it and must have thought I didn't want it as he took it away again. I padded my feet to remind him I was there and I'd missed his food share. He reached down again with food and made nice talking noises. But just as I went to take the food he took it back again. There was much yapping noise from the rest of his pack so I joined in to show I wanted to be part of them. Their yapping grew louder and the man with the food reached to the ground to pick something up. Maybe food he'd dropped? He threw it at me but I couldn't catch it and it hit my side, hurting me. I looked to see what it was but it wasn't food, it was a stone. I felt another one strike me and then another hit my head. I ran away as the pack yelping grew in pitch and volume.

Still hungry and now hurting from the boot and the stones I found a corner in the small tree place and curled into as tight a ball as I could against the coming cold night. Halfway through the night the rain started and I pushed myself as far under one of the small trees as I could, tucking my nose into my front paws. The rain continued and the cold started to hurt.

***

When the sun came again the warmth seeped into my aching body, soothing yesterday's bruises. It was early in the new day and few humans were around. One lady sat at the tables. I did my best stare and she shared a tiny piece of her food with me. It was sweet and crunchy but very very small. Just enough to remind me how hungry I was. I waited but she opened her hands at me to show she had no more food, even for herself, so I wandered off.

I found Bin Diver in a side street just off the plaza. He'd been in one of the big square boxes and brought out lots of paper and stuff. Muddled in with the paper was small bits of food. I looked at him and waited until he said I could join in. Together we scuffled through the paper taking every tiny bite we could find. Bin Diver went into the box several times looking for more, bring different items out each time for us to examine more closely. But despite the food-like smells coming from the big box we could find no more. A loud barking from two humans nearby caught our attention. We looked up and saw the humans were coming towards us with long sticks in their hands. They weren't play sticks and although these humans didn't move very quickly they still looked dangerous. We split up and ran in different directions.

My morning search of the usual places had given me no food today and by the time the sun was at its highest I was so hungry my stomach hurt so I decided to risk the area with the tables again. I noticed the two humans from the day before, the lady with the covered legs. She hadn't shared much yesterday but it had been a little bit at least and they hadn't thrown stones or kicked. I sat and waited, staring at her. At first they didn't see me as they continued to make their quiet human talking noises across the table. Some of the noises I recognised, funny little sounds that reminded me of something very important. I knew these noises. What did they mean?

Suddenly she saw me and gave me the eye shapes of recognition. I returned the expression to show I recognised her also. She made a high pitched talking noise and gave me meat. I chewed then licked her fingers. Once more I tasted that strangely familiar scent, this time it seemed stronger, more recognisable but I still couldn't place it. All the humans I'd met in my short life smelled and tasted slightly differently, it seemed odd to find a scent that was familiar but still unrecognisable.

I heard a low growl behind me and turned to look. Fierce One stared at me with narrowed eyes and teeth bared. His huge shoulders were hunched and he looked ready to leap. Fierce One is well known to all who live round here, he is violent and unpredictable. I put my tail down and my ears back to show I wasn't going to accept his challenge and that I acknowledged his status. I scuttered between the legs of the humans knowing Fierce One was too big to follow then I ran faster than a cat through the tables and down a side street. I went many doorways before I risked stopping to see if he was coming. As I'd expected, he wasn't interested in chasing me, he just wanted me away from the humans with food so he could take it for himself. This was going to be another hungry day.

Evening came and the skies darkened too quickly with the threat of much rain. The humans seemed to know it was coming and the plaza became empty of all but us street dogs and a couple of the noisy men. I needed food. Sometimes humans put bags of stuff outside their homes at night, usually bottles and cardboard but occasionally there's some food in them. The narrow streets are best for this so I made may way down one that I know is usually quiet. I found one of the bags, it was already open so I guessed the cats had been there before me. Still, they might have left something, they're more fussy than I am. I scratched and pulled at the bag, spreading the contents around to release the smells and have a better view. There was nothing much there although one of the plastic pieces smelled and tasted of blood. I chewed at it trying to gain what strength it would give.

I was so engrossed in my mission of chewing the plastic that I didn't hear the approaching pack until it was too late. They leapt at me from the dark and the rain, many of them. We tumbled and fought and I tried to use the skills that Hunter had taught me but there were too many. I didn't even have the chance to escape as they corralled me into a tight corner before taking turns to spring and attack. I tried turning on my back to show surrender but they just kept on coming. Eventually they slowed then grouped into a close pack staring down at me. This was their signal that I should now leave and never return to their land. I turned and struggled away.

***

The coming daylight did little to warm me. My coat smelled of blood and as I tried to clean the wounds more blood began to flow. My tongue filled with the taste of blood, mud and caked grit and in the end I gave up and let sleep take me.

I awoke once more when the sun was high which meant I'd missed the best scavenging time. I tried to move but my legs wouldn't work properly and I was so tired. Darkness stole over my vision once more and next time I woke the sun was well into its last cycle for the day. This time my legs cooperated a bit better and I made my way sluggishly into the plaza. The place with the tables was busy but I kept my distance as I scanned the area. Fierce One was the other side of the tables, watching closely for humans with food. I had no strength left for more fights. I was about to go back to the place of the small trees when I heard the nice humans, the ones with the gentle talking noises. I turned to see them approaching across the plaza. I might just be in luck, if they were going to the tables I might get a feed today after all. They came close and stood by the tables for a moment then started to move away. No! I risked exposing myself and tried to follow them but everything hurt so much that all I really wanted to do was lie down and sleep the big sleep. I was losing them. I shouted. As loud as I could I shouted. I knew I risked attracting the attention of Fierce One but I had nothing else.

The nice humans stopped and turned. They looked around for a moment without seeing me, I'm still small. Then the lady with the covered legs made the eye shapes of recognition and gave one of her high pitched talking sounds. She moved towards me with her front paws out to me. I wagged my tail as much as the pain would allow and returned the eye shapes of recognition. She came down to my size with lots and lots of very soft talking sounds. I felt myself being wrapped up in her paws then lifted into the air. Sleep took away the rest of the happening.

***

I awoke in the warm. Everything smelled different yet at the same time oddly familiar. I heard talking noises and turned my head slowly. The nice humans were sitting nearby and watching me. They made excited talking when they saw me lift my head. I tried to stand to go over to them but there was something wrong with my back legs. I twisted to look and saw they were wrapped in a cloth so tight I couldn't move them properly. I tugged at the cloth with my teeth, it wouldn't come off. The lady with the covered legs came close, and made herself small like me. She brushed my head and back with her paw, making very soft talking noises as she did so. It was soothing and comforting and I remembered this.

The days cycled and they kept me in the warm and soft place except for the few times I needed to go outside. They gave me so much food that I even had to stop eating at one point. I remembered the taste of their food and the smells of their house, the sounds and the shapes. Would they remember?

As I explored more of their house I found more things I knew. I found one of my balls on the top of one of their big brown boxes. It was next to a flat image of a dog. A big dog, much bigger than me. I managed to reach my ball, it was much bigger in my mouth than I remember. I took it to the lady with the covered legs to show her what I'd found. She made very loud talking noises I didn't understand and narrowed her eyes in challenge. I dropped the ball at her feet and she made a loud very high pitched sound then water came from her eyes. The nice man came in and they wrapped their paws around each other, the lady still making funny whelping noises. They made talking noises muddled in with the funny whelping sound but suddenly I recognised one of the sounds.

"Saxon." I knew that sound. That was the sound that once made me come to my people... before... before. Before what?

I told them I knew that noise but they took no notice and went into a different room and closed the door. I listened to their talking noises, humans are easy to hear even when they are trying not to be heard. I heard another sound I remembered, "Jan." But I couldn't remember what the sound was for. Was it a pack call? Maybe.

It was when I found my old collar that I had the biggest feeling of remembering, but also much strangeness. This was certainly my collar, bright red with shiny bits around it and a circular shiny bit hanging underneath. It still even had my faint smells. But it was so big! I'd found it when I'd managed to climb onto another one of those big brown boxes. This particular brown box was tall and I'd only managed to reach the top by climbing on one of their seats. The top of the box had many other shiny things I didn't know. Some of them fell to the floor as I retrieved my collar. Tinkling crashing sounds they made as they tumbled.

I took my collar to my bed and put it next to my ball then curled up with them. My people came in, probably the crashing noise had made them curious. The lady looked at me and made another high pitched noise and kept making it until the man put his paws around her. I stood up and told them who I was but they weren't listening. I told them again and again but still they took no notice. Then I had an idea. I remembered another box. A box where my people kept the things they put on their lower paws. The lady kept some very soft ones in there, ones she only wore when she was inside. I went to find the box. It was still where I'd remembered only being much smaller now it was very difficult to open and find one of the soft paw covers. In the end I actually managed to get inside whereas before I'd been able to open it fully. I clambered around and found one of them, the smell was strong here and I remembered more. I remembered what I used to do. I picked up the soft thing and ran back into the other room with it.

My people were sitting together in the big seat. I jumped up before they realised what I was doing and I dropped the soft paw cover on the lady's legs. She made very big eyes. Scared eyes. I wondered what I'd done to frighten her so badly, I just wanted to show her. Water came to her eyes again and she stared at me, making those funny whelping noises. I was frightened. Had I

45

done something that would get me taken away again? I whimpered and snuggled as close as I could to show her how much I loved her. I buried my nose into the folds of her body covering. It was warm and safe and smelled of home, of my pack. Please don't let me go away again. I risked a look.

Her eyes made the recognition shape as they ran with water.

"Saxon?" she said.

Me and Mrs. Jones – Not civil to the Guardia

By David Bull

Me and Mrs. Jones – Not civil to the Guardia

By David Bull

It had all started so well. A sunny afternoon, me putting up a fence in the garden while Mrs Jones and Meg soaked up some rays. Then the Guardia turned up. At first it wasn't clear what exactly I'd done wrong to deserve the presence of two officers of the crown at my gate, but here they were.

Apparently someone had smashed into a car and left the scene pretty rapidly, forgetting to fill out the accident form and disappearing into the distance. Apparently, that someone was me.

Now at this point they asked to see my car, so I showed them. 'No, the other car,' said one of them with very bushy eyebrows (I actually wondered how he could see me but I bet they are handy in the summer…). I offered the (honest) excuse that I didn't have another but (apparently) I had acquired a BMW (black) with significant frontal damage. It didn't matter what I said they insisted that I must have hidden it somewhere…all this was getting hard to take, especially with his eyebrows moving up and down as he talked.

Eventually, they agreed to look at my ID and realised that my name, and the guy's they were looking for, were completely different. At last, some common sense was going to prevail (I thought) but I was on another train of thought completely to eyebrows and his mate. My ID was false. It was checked, by phone, by radio all they failed to do was hold it up to my face and compare but they were not having it. Despite my protestations I was heading for the cooler (I know but it's the only way I can get my name in the same sentence as Steve McQueen…) and arrangements were made (by them) for me to be taken away.

My knights in shining armour turned out to be the Local Police, who arrived in the nick (geddit?) of time and called me 'Dave,' I almost replied

48

with an 'I love you' as eyebrows whipped his head between the two of us lost in the confusion. My friendly boys in blue began a serious sounding, although I could only hear whispers, conversation, about me. The looks over the shoulder from all the officers were still unnerving; especially eyebrows and I began to worry for my future once again. Stripy pyjamas are just not me, especially the ones with arrows on. Anyway, to keep a long story long, it turned out that I didn't have a BMW, hadn't crashed and legged it and I was, in fact, the bloke that it said I was. Bit like Ronseal really. So everyone was happy once again, although eyebrows and co' didn't offer an apology but they did shake my hand over the gate.

It was that point that Mrs Jones decided to put in an appearance and put her front paws on the top of the gate – eyeballing eyebrows – and then it happened. To give him credit he took it well and returned to his car without another word. Mrs Jones, for her part, had let out the longest belch I've heard from any animal, let alone a Great Dane, into his face. It was compounded by the noise of her cheeks rattling against her gums by the force of the escaping air, and Eyebrows' er, eyebrows being pushed against his forehead.

I don't expect Eyebrows to hold a grudge, but just in case, if anyone can bake a nice jam sponge, with a file in it…

Cassidy

By Kirsten Rose

Cassidy

By Kirsten Rose

She was the love of my life. We met when I passed her in a pet store window. I swore I would never buy a dog from a pet store when so many needed homes from the rescue centres, and I know now that the industry is appalling, but there I was at 23 and there she was, completely unaware of any of my ideals. She just needed a home. We named her Cassidy, of Grateful Dead origins, and picked her out of the lovely litter of Rottweiler/Black Lab puppies because, well, she came to us full of fire and fun and drew blood when she bit Tommy's finger. He insisted this meant she wanted to come home with us. I couldn't think of any better reason, so we began our love affair.

After two years I thought, ok, this is starting to be manageable. She was the feistiest critter I'd ever met. After a year of struggling with her wildness, we tried classes that I thought were somehow "humane" because they use those spiffy Gentle Leader thingies instead of a throat-choking collar. I liked it ok, but after we got the basic idea of "please don't run away from me into the road" and "stop when I really need you to" I couldn't really bring myself to force my agenda on her freedom. That was good enough for us.

By the time she reached four years old, she was by far The Coolest Canine I had ever met. She was smart, funny, fast, playful, snuggly, intuitive, and a wonderful presence in my family life. Her one big down side was she was also a Dumpster Diva. This name was given to her by a friend after yet another long day waiting for her to return home after a runaway moment, stomach distended, portending days of strange things coming out of her bum as they made their way through her digestive system (tinfoil, plastic wrap, bones, and other assorted horrors). I know, I know, how could I let my girl just run free in the neighbourhood? The neighbours must have been so annoyed with the tipped over rubbish bins, but there were hardly any cars and we were in the middle of a national forest area. Anyway, one day she came home while I was making lunch and entered the kitchen absolutely reeking of rotten garbage. I took one look at her and in my typically dramatic fashion said "You Stink! Get out of my kitchen!" She went out onto the porch and I didn't think anything more of it, until a moment later she came back in behind me completely covered in the delicious scent of lavender. She had gone out onto the porch and rubbed her head all over in the lavender bush. From this moment on, I knew I was living with an enlightened soul!

We lived in North Lake Tahoe, California, one of the most beautiful places in the world. It was a wonderful place to be a dog, and a person, and lots of other things. There is far more open forest, woods, water, rivers, running-about-without-a-collar space than anywhere I've been, and Cassidy loved it. There wasn't much need for an obedient dog, and as she got a little older, we came to a beautiful understanding... you just stay out of the road, and make me look good by coming when I call, and I'll let you run as free as you like all the days of your life (or so I thought). And it was heavenly. She kept me up and out, hiking and running and swimming and all things healthy, EVERY day! It was good for both of us, body and soul.

Like so many dogs, when she started to age, she just didn't get it. She didn't have some sense that told her she should slow down. I had a roommate who was wild about mountain biking and hiking and would take Cassidy on walks and bike rides. One day she came back and Cassidy could hardly walk. Oh my dear girl... what has she done? "Well, she just kept going" said the roommate. OF COURSE, I thought... have you MET my dog? What would she do? Lay down in the middle of the trail and declare she is going no further? From that day forward, things began to change, I think the phrase is "going downhill." She was moving beyond middle age and entering the upper years where grey hairs were popping out attractively around her muzzle, and she wasn't jumping up so quickly when it was time for a walk.

But I wasn't quite giving up on her best days, so after a lot of doggie chiropractic, acupuncture and massage, she was moving just fine and had a lot of joyful walks left in her. Then I dropped the bomb. "In your senior years, the supposed best and most peaceful of your days, we are moving to Los Angeles." I considered if it would be better to leave her with a dear friend in the glorious mountains of Tahoe, and quickly felt the guilty pain of even having had the thought. We were a team and there was no way she would be happier without me, even in the mountains.

Cassidy had been with me longer and more intimately than any other person, place or thing in my entire life, including my parents. She was with me when I got married, and with me when I got divorced. She was with me when I worked at the Domestic Violence shelter, and laid with me as I came home crying about the state of the world. She made me laugh, and licked my face when I cried. She was the big sister to her little puppy brother Mingus, and when he died after only 9.5 years, I told her she had to give me at least 2 more years before she left me or I couldn't possibly handle it. And so she did... almost 2 years to the date.

She was nearing 14 when I started sneaking her into my new job teaching in a high school. When she was younger, I had worked where I could take her with me, and now, in her tender elder years, there she was at home alone (in the trees and beauty, but nonetheless alone) with me overwhelmed in a classroom filled with teenagers every day, wishing I could be with her instead, wondering how I had gotten us so far from the gentle life we knew in the mountains. So, I snuck her in. I told these rambunctious, annoying, teasing, wonderful teenagers to keep a secret.

We were in a "temporary" outbuilding with just two classrooms, as far away from the main buildings as could be on campus. The administrators never came by and neither did anyone else for that matter. The kind teacher next door wasn't going to give me away, and now I had to count on 5 classes filled with 35-40 kids each class to also not give me away. How we did it, I don't know, but somehow for the last two months of school they kept my secret, and fell almost as in love with Cassidy as I was. Her wizened grey beard was so fitting for the wise old being she had become. People just looked at her and felt they were in the presence of someone really special. The students felt honoured if she gave them extra attention, let them pet her or laid by their desks. It was good for everyone, but the boss probably wouldn't have thought so. She didn't like me much. And so they kept our secret.

The next school year I moved to a different school (yes, getting away from the boss who didn't like me very much), and it was no longer an option to bring Cassidy into my class. However, every morning, I awoke at 4:44 a.m. (it just seemed more fun than 4:45) and did my morning sadhana of yoga and breathing while Cass continued to sleep. After breakfast she would slowly get herself up, looking up at me with her beautiful brown eyes saying "Alright then, let's get to work if we must". I would load her up onto the nice futon bed I had in the back of my big car and park her under a big shady tree. I came out at my breaks and spent my free block (supposedly for class planning) walking slowly with her, or just laying down for a while. Near the end, she couldn't walk very well and I had to carry her up and down stairs. Thankfully she had lost a bit of her usual 90 pounds in her old age, and there weren't too many stairs in our life. She also now only wanted to walk enough to go for a wee and poo.

At this point, my entire world was revolving around taking care of her, just as we started approaching Christmas break. We had two+ weeks off and I was so happy Cassidy had made it this far. Every day had started to be a rush through time, rushing my classes so I could get back to her, wondering how I might find her. Then, once our vacation started, I didn't have to ever leave her alone for what felt like the approaching end.

Cassidy was clearly dying. I had taken her into the vet, who sadly suggested the most humane thing would be to put her to sleep. I couldn't fathom how that was humane? It seemed unnatural and only there to make my life more convenient in not caretaking a dying friend. So we went away and carried on with our last days together.

Our days often consisted of driving down to the beach and parking with the back open to the Pacific Ocean so she could watch the waves and surfers and smell the sea air. Christmas time in Los Angeles can be delightful and warm so we enjoyed a lot of sunshine together. She was beyond wanting to get out and run about, and she seemed pleased to sniff the air and peacefully lay with me. Some days we just hung out at the house and sat out on the porch together, looking at the mountains. I lived in Topanga Canyon and we had a wonderful little studio with big windows and wonderful views and many animal visitors- mice, opossum, deer, rattlesnakes, hawks, doves, and who knows what else. It was peaceful and I was never more connected with her and the magic of the natural world around me than when sitting on that porch during her transition time. Every ant, every breath, was magic. Time somehow slowed down and shared some of its secrets.

As Christmas day approached, the entire world outside seemed to disappear. Friends came by to check on us, but I wasn't up for chatting. I really couldn't spend any energy that was not with Cassidy, and the thinning veils between our worlds to wherever we go when we die were becoming

54

thinner and we were both becoming part of the beyond. I could hear and feel her every breath like it was my own. I wrote a lullaby for her that I played often those days.

Go to sleep, my little baby next to me
I will hold you while you dream of the sweet things your next life will bring
And when I wake up in the morning and you're by my side baby still alive,
I cry, and give thanks for another day
And if in the night the time seems right for your heart and soul to take their
flight to the light
I know love will lead you on
And when I'm sad cause you're leaving and not coming back
I just sit by the sea and remember you're always here with me

Two days before Christmas, we started staying in the back of the car most of the time, just getting up to go to the bathroom. We had a wonderful big bed there and we were both quite happy with our views, the delicious mountains and fresh sea air rolling up the canyon, though I could see she was leaving me more and more, further than I could follow her. I would go up to the house to make myself food now and again, though Cassidy was done with eating. Christmas Eve night I barely slept a wink, though not for the reasons I had in childhood anticipating of the presents in the morning. This anticipation was different. Her breath was getting softer and softer, and I spent my time hoping for each inhale to come again.

Then on Christmas Day, I suddenly saw a disgusting sight. There were tiny worm-like things floating around in her eyes. Oh my God, I thought, maybe she just has worms! And somehow I was excited by the idea, what if we could FIX this?? Like a ridiculous, desperate lover, I raced her to the emergency room at a wonderful hospital in Ventura. The doctor there was so kind, and really could see how desperate I was... my best friend was dying and I thought I might have just gotten a "Get Out of Jail Free" card. So with gentleness she told me the worms had nothing to do with her dying, they were just moving in a bit early. I should go home and be still with her.

Ugh. I beat myself for a while about that one. What an uncomfortable journey that must have been, bumping around in the back on her deathbed. She really wasn't aware of too much as she was already half-way crossing, yet still I felt sad about the rushing about into the hospital where she lay on a

55

hard table with a stranger poking about her, no matter how kind she was, just to confirm that, indeed, Cassidy was dying and there was nothing to be done.

So we got home and it was Christmas night. I now hadn't slept much for 2 days and the night was approaching. We snuggled up together in the back of the car, and as hard as I tried to stay awake to be with her, I fell into a deep slumber.

I have heard many times that the dying often wait to die until their loved ones leave the room, go home for a shower, or out for a quick walk to stretch their legs. Perhaps they want their own bit of peace in the final moment, or maybe it is just too hard to let go when the living are holding on so strongly. I was definitely willing Cassidy alive. As much as I was telling with my words that I would be ok and she could leave, that is not what my heart was saying. My heart was saying "Please don't leave me. You are the best friend I have ever had. You have watched me grow up into a woman, and now I don't know who I will be without you". And so she waited until I was deeply asleep.

Out of the depths of sleep, out of the chasm of the dark void, out of the space where all energy comes and must return, I was called back sharply into my body, like a bell was ringing me awake. In that very moment I heard a deep exhale. Oh my God – I fell asleep and she is gone. Then a slow inhale. What's happening? And exhale. And slower still. The tears are falling, my heart is breaking and my girl is leaving. The final breath came... and went... the constant soundtrack to my life for 14 years was changed to complete silence. I looked at the clock. It was 4:44 a.m. The hour of the angels. The hour of my final goodbye. She was gone.

I left her head on her soft pillow and I covered her with the most beautiful blanket we had, a hand embroidered, white blanket and put lavender flowers on top. She looked beautiful with her salt and pepper hair against that blanket. And I left her there for a day of mourning. She looked so peaceful.

And there is was. My dearest friend who had given me more joy, more peace, more fun and more love than I had known in my life, was gone. I was grateful I still had a week before needing to go back to school. The transition was great. My life which used to have the steady heartbeat of two was now solitary. I think I was numb for quite some time. I went back to school and tried to get on with life.

About a month after Cassidy left, I drove home one dark winter's night after a long day at school. I was tired, the sky was clear, and the beauty in

56

that clear, starry sky was breathtaking. I sat in my car, and suddenly she was there. For a moment, her being filled me completely with peace and knowing. I began to cry. Now I was truly alone. The feelings I had been keeping under the surface were arising under this watchful benevolence. It was like I could hear her then, through the sobbing, through the loneliness, through the gasping breaths, "You are never alone, you are never alone". And for the first time, this idea that I have heard and thought was becoming real. In letting in the despair of utter loneliness I found I really am not alone.

It has taken me this long to even begin to consider that there may be another canine companion in my life. When Cassidy died, people immediately said "Are you going to get another dog?" like I could simply go out and replace the pain of losing my beloved friend of 14 years by getting a new puppy. "No," I said, "she was irreplaceable."

Life is much different now. Cassidy helped me grow up. With both her and Mingus gone, I started my new life, the one where I find out new corners of who I really am. I left teaching, left LA, and began travelling the world, which I had always wanted to do. Along the way I met my husband, and we now live in Orgiva, Spain with our delicious 4 yr old son. We are still moving about a bit, but the first thing I will do when we find our own home is to put an invitation out to the universe to send us our new canine companion. Then I'll settle in for the ride!

Daphne's Story

By Francesca Stewart

Daphne's Story

By Francesca Stewart

My name is Francesca Stewart and these are my personal views on animal cruelty and what I and many others are trying to do to end this pain and suffering.

This story takes place in 2015, a time when not all animals were being treated fairly, where the world didn't treat animals the way they deserved. Dogs would go unfed, beaten, and left to die, and people like you and I lived the good life, we had everything we wanted and lived in the happiness of being the dominant species. I believe that the world should be a place where animals and people are equal. After all we did descend from animals, so surely we should look up to them? Animals should have all the same rights as us. Now clearly dogs can't drive cars or build houses, but shouldn't they have respect, love, food, and support? I'm not saying that all dogs don't get this, because a lot do, but in all countries many dogs are abused and people need to put an end to it. Animals walk the streets alone at night needing some food or shelter, whilst we are fast asleep in our nice warm home. This is the 21st century, we have planes, cars and millionaires but can't we just stop and think about the things that really need fixing, poverty, illness, and animal abuse?

Now you may think why am I going on about this? Well Daphne has inspired me to write about this, she has given me a big eye-opener to the dogs in this world and that it must change now.

I'm not just talking about dogs in certain places, rich, poor, English, Italian, it doesn't matter where you are from or what you believe, it's what is done that matters, so many things can be done to help these animals, donations, or just care, maybe you have a pet? Would you beat it? Starve it? Abuse it? I could go on and complain for hours, but the main question is;

would you like this done to you? No? That's what I thought. If you saw a young child out on the street with no food or water, in pain, and broken? Would you help them? Yes! People think that just because it's a child not an animal it makes them more 'important' no, no it doesn't. Yes we should help every child, but why can't we show some respect for animals too?

I have a dog called Daphne, she is only two, she's very small, and has the resemblance of a sausage dog but with a Jack Russell face, black with small patches of brown and a white chin. She was found walking the streets of Spain, homeless with two puppies, starving close to death. She was taken into a place in Spain like a kennel. In the UK we have laws to ensure that all animals in animal rescue centres are being helped and loved and no harm is coming to them. But in Spain things aren't quite the same.

Some kennels are horrible, lots of all sizes of dogs are put into pens and are free to attack each other and fight. Before we were planning on taking Daphne, we found a dog called Ella. she was found in a terrible state, with hair that was so overgrown that you couldn't even tell which breed she was. We raised the money to have Ella taken out. It was her last night in the pen and she was

attacked by a bigger dog, so badly hurt that she later on died. Is this right? No, dog should have to go through such trauma. She probably would have been safer on the streets, but because she was in these kennels with dangerous dogs, she was killed. In some ways the death wasn't anyone's fault but in others it was. If she and all the other dogs were in their own pens they wouldn't be free to fight, which is why in the UK animals don't share pens.
Ella.

Daphne came from a bad background where she was probably beaten. This was shown later on when she wouldn't go near men, and became extremely nervous. When her and her two young puppies were put into the kennels, they sat in the corner scared, she is a very small dog, and when it came to meal time, all they did was put a bowl of food in the middle of the kennel and let them battle for the food. Now clearly the biggest dogs got in first and the smallest dogs like Daphne were left with nothing. So this meant that small dogs like Daphne didn't have food, and each day in these horrible conditions it got harder and harder for them to survive.

Luckily for Daphne there's a small charity in Spain that goes into these kennels and takes pictures of them, they are then posted on social media pages and shown for adoption, of course her puppies were gone first, two cute puppies gone to a good home, meaning Daphne was left alone to defend herself. Then my mum, who got introduced to the charity by her auntie, saw the photos of Daphne. Before we could even bring her home we had to pay £60 to get her out of the kennels and into a foster home until she was able to be brought to this country for a further amount of £250. The woman who runs this charity has a van that her husband drives, taking each of these dogs to their new homes. They made the journey as nice as they could for the dogs but of course it was still a long and traumatic experience for them.

Now after going through all of this, Daphne finally got to us, frightened scared and panicked. It normally takes a dog a week or so to settle into their home, but it took Daphne about two months to finally feel slightly safe in our home. She wouldn't go anywhere near men, she found it difficult to be away from her puppies, being alone, and most of all she found it most unusual to be cared for, to have regular meals and a warm bed. If you ever went to pet her, she would panic and get so nervous that she would wee herself or run into a corner. She became attached to my mum, running to her like a safety blanket. Even five months on, if anyone new comes over, or goes near her she panics, and will be frightened.

We have three dogs already, Lola a small white fluffy Chihuahua cross Maltese, Billy a Jack Russell cross and Cyril another Jack Russell cross. All three are very friendly dogs. The morning of Daphne's arrival, we let her out into the garden. Even being around dogs her own size and smaller, the trauma of being in the kennels had made her panic being around dogs that she thought could bring harm to her. And being without her puppies around, new dogs were a scary experience. But now Daphne has got used to being around these dogs and realising they were going to do no harm to her, she has become the leader of the pack. Playing and bossing them all around. Even though Daphne has become used to being around my dogs, going for walks is still a scary thing, passing strange dogs that she's never seen before. When Daphne and Lola play together you can really see they have different personalities, Lola is such a loud and brave dogs, will go up to anyone with leaps of happiness, but Daphne just slowly follows along, hiding in the shadows afraid and worried, or what's around the corner.

In Spain dogs are all over the streets, like we have birds here in the UK, they often get run over running in front of cars, as do birds in this country.

Do people stop and help birds or squirrels in this country? No they just carry on driving. At times, in Spain if someone ran over a dog they would just leave it and keep on driving. I'm not saying you should help a dog and not a bird, but why? Surely people should stop the over population of dogs in that country and make their laws stricter. If Spain and other countries had the laws and support to help they could have places such as the RSPCA to stop all this pain? This is why people need to act on this now and save poor dogs such as Daphne. Even with everything she's been through, to have the life she has now, she's one of the lucky ones.

Even though Daphne has a new and transformed life, she can never forget the pain and uncomfortable life that she's left behind. Knowing all the pain she's been through, just makes me think about what sort of people could do this to her? Why would they do it? What must have been going through their head to hurt such a beautiful little dog? She will never be completely comfortable to go up to a new person, she will always be a shy dog. Only five months on will she comfortably come up to me. For someone to abuse a poor innocent dog, in such horrific ways, is sickening, and should make anyone who has ever hurt a dog feel ashamed. But Daphne is one of millions of dogs in this world being badly hurt, and not just in Spain but all over the world. Some dogs are put in even worse situation. It just makes me wonder why people would have dogs just to hurt them. I wrote about this to make people aware of what's going on and how Daphne opened my eyes to it. I hope this shows people that dogs deserve a good loving home. Dogs like Daphne have done nothing wrong in this world and all they deserve is love and kindness.

When Daphne was in the kennel, they would slowly become full as more and more dogs were put in. once it became full, they would have to kill the dogs. In the UK we have the medicine to put animals to sleep, pain free. But in Spain they aren't as lucky as us, they sometimes get killed it unthinkable ways, that's why Daphne is one of the lucky dogs that got out of there before this could have happened to her.

Andalucía and Murcia in Spain are big tourist attractions, the perfect summer holiday, with bars and pubs and beautiful beaches, but there is a dark side to this that people don't seem to know about dogs walk the streets looking for food in the bars and pubs, and now and again they get a bit of food. One cause of the overpopulation of dogs comes from hunters who abandon their dogs after hunting season. They breed them, use them and then either kill them or leave them on the streets. Not only are they badly treated but they are then left, battered and bruised with nowhere to go. When these dogs wander into these pubs the staff sometimes call the pound to come and collect them, which they then very often die. When it comes to the next year of hunting, they just breed new dogs and they also get abandoned once the hunting is over. The same thing happens every year.

My mum's auntie Caroline has lived in Spain for ten years and she been helping animals since the day she's been there, fostering and aiding dogs, taking them in and picking them up off the streets. She has always loved Spain and has wanted to live there, when she finally got the chance it was a dream come true and now the only thing that would make her want to come back to the UK would be that she can't stand to see the poor dogs being treated in this way, it pains her to see them like this day in and out. Me, her and thousands of other people around the world who are helping this charity agree that new laws need to be enforced and the government needs to address this problem, it's not fair dogs are treated this way and the change needs to happen now, for this to end and for a new look upon animal cruelty need to be seen.

If Spain didn't have charities like the one that helped Daphne, thousands of dogs would be walking the streets, without a home. Even though the charity is doing an amazing job to help these dogs, they need help, maybe even your help? But of course not just in Spain but in all other parts of the world. Governments need to address these problems and support these animals, the world needs to work together to improve the real issues and bring it to an end, no longer should an animal go without a loving home or a good quality of life or love and care. Just stop and think, we're not the only things on this planet and it should be addressed to the next generation, to show them they shouldn't follow in these footsteps. Change it now before it's too late.

Me and Daphne today.

Jack's Story

By Leonora Finch

Jack's Story

By Leonora Finch

My name is Jack and I live outside most of the time, guarding my owner's coal yard. I wear a collar with a chain attached, so I can't move very far and it's very boring. My owner doesn't seem to like me very much as I am supposed to be fierce and frighten people away, but I am always pleased to see everyone and wag my tail in delight.

One day my owner appears with another man who is wearing a uniform. He looks very smart and makes me feel a little afraid at first, but then he bends down to pat me and I see he has very kind eyes. I wag my tail and lick his hands. "You can see why I don't want him," my owner says, "He's useless as a guard dog. If you don't want him, he'll be on a one way trip to the vets." My owner and this new man talk for a few minutes and then this new kind man fastens a lead to my collar, ridding me of my hateful chain and takes me away from the only home I have ever known. He takes me to a truck and we travel for a long time. It's dark when the truck stops and I am then taken to a row of kennels that contain lots of other dogs. They come to the gates of their pens to see the new arrival. I am saddened to think that I am going to be confined again in this new kennel, but when I am inside I find a comfortable bed and after a little while the nice man who rescued me brings a tasty bowl of food, so I begin to be happier. Lots of the other dogs are barking, but I am quite content to curl up and sleep.

The next morning the nice kind man comes to collect me and I am taken, along with several of the other dogs to a big field, surrounded by trees. I don't know what I am supposed to do at first, but over the next few weeks I am taught lots of new things and I am really enjoying this new life. I am becoming very fond of "the kind man" and know he is called Jim. I spend all day with him and he always seems to be very pleased with me. I spend most days with a back pack strapped to me and then I am sent off to find people that are hiding in the woods. It all seems very strange to me. These people are always very pleased when I find them. Also while I am doing this there are lots of loud noises going on, which I find frightening at first, but I soon get used to it. It really is like one big game. I would have been quite happy to spend the rest of my life doing this, but one day everything changes. I sense the anxiety of everyone around me. Lorries are being loaded and everyone is in a great hurry. I do not like this. Am I going to be separated from my wonderful friend Jim, I wonder. I cower in my kennel and wait. After what seems ages, I am taken out of my pen with several of the other dogs. My heart is beating rapidly, I am very anxious. We are loaded onto a lorry. There is lots of noise, dogs barking and men shouting.

Our journey is short and we arrive at a strange place, where I can smell the sea. A huge ship is nearby. I see horses being lifted on to this ship in big slings, they are screaming in fright. I am so scared, if only Jim was with me. Amazingly, in answer to my prayers he appears by the lorry. He fastens my lead and takes me towards the big ship, all the while making a fuss of me. Immediately I feel relief flooding through my body. I know Jim will look after me. Hundreds of men are boarding this ship. Many have dogs and we are all herded together, jostling and pushing against each other, but I don't mind. I am with Jim and I feel safe. We eventually manage to find a quiet corner on the ship and Jim and I hunker down. He feeds me some of the food he has been given and talks soothingly to me. Around us men are joking and laughing together and some are playing cards and smoking. We pass the next few hours pleasantly enough and I curl up and snooze for most of our journey. Then the atmosphere changes again. Our ship has stopped moving. I feel the tension from all the men around us. What is happening now, I think. Again we are jostled and pushed as we all head towards the gang planks and slowly disembark. I see many horses being unloaded, mules and donkeys. Crates of pigeons are stacked one on top of the other, by the harbour side. What is happening I ask myself. I follow Jim and know he will look after me. Hundreds of men are gathering together. We form a huge line. Jim is loaded down with a large rucksack and rifle, he wears a tin hat. Even I have a bag strapped to my back filled with things that need to be carried. We set off in a convoy. A strange mix of animals, men and machinery. We stop by the roadside occasionally to eat and rest.

At first spirits are high, but as the day drags on the men are tired and beginning to stumble. I nudge Jim's hand and wish I could help him with his heavy load. When darkness falls we reach some woods and all about us men begin to settle down for the night. I snuggle up to Jim and keep him warm. The next day, off we go again. After several hours, I begin to hear distant loud noises. *What is happening now*, I think? I am a little afraid again. So many strange things have been happening over the past few days. We arrive at a small, dilapidated looking village. Men are hurrying about, lorries are coming and going. This is to become our new home.

Over the next few weeks I begin to realise what all my former training has been about. Only this time it is for real. Horrendous battles are raging a short distance from our village. The sounds are deafening. When the worst of this horrendous noise is over, I wait with Jim in a very deep trench and then on his command, I am up and out of our refuge. Once again I am looking for bodies, but this time I am staggering through thick mud, there are clouds of smoke I struggle to see through and an acrid smell fills my lungs. I know this is not a game now, for many of the bodies I find smell different as they are dead. Grotesque in their terrible deaths. All life has flown from their broken bodies. I quickly sense the bodies that are still alive and seek them out. They are so glad to see me. I carry medicines in my back pack to relieve their pain and bandages to patch up their wounds. Sometimes Jim is with me and can help these poor men. Other times when it is too dangerous I go alone.

Up and down I patrol, helping whoever I can and then I return to the deep dark trenches. They are very often water logged and very unpleasant. Makeshift meals are eaten here and men sleep standing up, all huddled together. We seem to spend hours and hours just waiting and then suddenly all hell is let loose and then the same grim pattern repeats itself.

Between these spells in the trenches, we return to our "village" and then there is a brief period of respite before we have to return again to our duties. During these rest phases the men try to relax. Smoking, reading, or just talking together, mostly about their lives at home. Anything to take their minds off the hell we all find ourselves in. Sometimes they even have a game of football. I rush around after them, as do some of the other dogs. The men laugh and shout at us. Other days when the weather is bad, we all huddle around the makeshift fires, trying to keep warm, the men reading their mail from home and writing back their replies. Life goes on day after day. One morning after more horrendous noise of fighting I am sent over the top again.

I move quickly as I know I must. I find myself close to someone. I stop, sniffing at this new person. His clothes smell different to me and I feel uneasy, but then hands are feeling for my fur. I do not recognise the strange words this man is uttering. He is hanging on to me tightly. I see his face is wet with tears and pain. I nestle into his body and lick away his tears. I stay with this man, while he clings to me. I smell the blood on him and know he is very badly injured, but I can do no more.

Where is Jim? He will be able to help. I stay with this strange smelling man for what seems ages and then again Jim is beside me, along with a couple of other men. One of them is calling me away from my charge. He seems angry with me and I don't understand what is going on. He raises his rifle and points it at the fallen man who is shaking now, imploring with his eyes, not to be shot. Someone is shouting "damn hun, shoot him." A furious argument then breaks out. Jim is trying to stop the angry man. He grabs the rifle from him. I am just about to get up and protect Jim, but as quick as it started the argument dies down. The angry man turns away, muttering to his companions and disappears into the gloom. Jim kneels down and feels for the injured man's pulse. He looks at his mangled body and shakes his head. He takes a syringe from my back pack and injects it into the man's arm. Within minutes the man's grasp on me is getting fainter and fainter. His eyes are closed, his breathing is shallower and then slowly, very slowly he seems to slip away, whilst muttering the words, "Mutti Mutti" and then I know he has gone and I rejoin Jim at his side. My duty is done. I know Jim has done a good thing and I lick his hands. Jim fondles my head and we return to our village.

On our way back we pass a pitiful sight. A horse laden down with a heavy load has got stuck in the mud and is floundering helplessly. Several men are trying to haul it out with ropes. It seems hopeless, the horse is squealing with fright. Its eyes are wild and it is foaming at the mouth. Jim joins the rescue party and they all pull as hard as their exhausted bodies will let them. At last, very slowly the horse begins to slither from the treacherous mud. Inch by inch he escapes from a terrible death. The men are triumphant, cheering and clapping each other on the back. One man drops to his knees beside the horse's head and urges the poor creature to get up, which with a lot of stumbling, the horse eventually does. "That a boy, Captain, I knew you could do it." The man has his arms around the horse's neck and I am so glad the ending is a happy one. The man turns to the others and says, "This horse is my life, he has kept me going for so long, I don't know what I would do without him." There is lots more hand shaking and back slapping and then we all go our separate ways.

Many more months pass and I marvel that Jim and I are both still alive. Many faces, man and beast have disappeared. One dark day Jim and I are once more in the trenches. I feel very uneasy as we wait. A heaviness fills my heart and I am afraid.

Then Jim gives me the command and I am up and over the top again, running here and there and sometimes crawling, my body shakes, bullets are firing all around me. I am bewildered. Where am I? I think to myself. Then the pain hits, thundering through me. What's happening? I fall to the ground, groaning. I look back and my body is a sea of blood. I whimper and long for Jim, but he is far away and won't know where I am. I know I will die and hope it is soon as my body is wracked with pain. I lie panting in the mud for what seems hours, drifting in and out of conscientiousness and then a familiar smell fills my lungs. My Jim is here. Feebly I raise my head and wag my tail. I try to lick his hands, but it is all in vain. A strange sensation comes over me. I am slipping away. Suddenly I am rising above my broken body. I am looking down upon it and see the full extent of my terrible injuries. My poor Jim is sobbing and cradling my limp form. I wish I could tell him all pain has left me and I feel such happiness. I want to tell him how grateful I am that he rescued me from my life in the coal yard and that he has taught me so much in our short time together. I also know and wish I could tell him, as I look down upon him, still cradling my poor body and weeping, that I will walk by his side forever.

This story is dedicated to all the dogs that lost their lives in the service of mankind.

Dogs had a vital part to play in World War One. It is estimated that by 1918, Germany had employed 30,000 dogs, Britain, France and Belgium over 20,000. Lots of dog breeds were used, the most popular type being medium sized, intelligent and trainable breeds. There were sentry dogs used for patrolling, scout dogs used for scouting ahead. These dogs could scent the enemy up to 1,000 yards away.

Jack was a casualty dog. Trained to find the injured and dying and equipped with medical supplies, these dogs would also stay with soldiers until they died.

Messenger dogs were also used and were as reliable as men in the dangerous job of running messages. These dogs were faster than a human runner, were less of a target to a sniper and could travel over any terrain and were extremely reliable.

Mascot dogs were also common and proved a great psychological comfort that helped the soldiers cope with the many horrors of war.

Jazz And The Restoration Of Harmony

By Craig Briggs

Jazz And The Restoration Of Harmony

By Craig Briggs

Trust and loyalty are the cornerstones of any lasting relationship and Jasmine had both in abundance.

We first met one another in July 1998 at the Halifax branch of the RSPCA. Described as a Collie-cross, she was a shy, young puppy about 18 months old. The fact that she was more, 'cross' than Collie didn't matter to us. We hit it off straight away and Jazz, or Badger as she was then known, became the dog for us.

A fresh start called for a new name. We tried all the old favourites, but not a twitch: the mother-in-law even suggested, "Ambulance". But dogs have a way of choosing their own name and when Jasmine was mentioned, she plumped for that.

'I'm not going out in public shouting Jasmine,' I protested. So Jasmine quickly became Jazz.

She soon settled in to her new home but the past of a rescue dog is hidden in their eyes and viewed through their behaviour. Jazz was terribly nervous, the slightest gust of wind or rustle of leaves would see her jump with fright.

From the security of the lounge she would bark ferociously at the sight of ladders, much to the amusement of the window cleaner, and the appearance of another man in the house would send her cowering beneath my legs. Progress was slow but little by little she began to trust others.

When granny had a spell in hospital, Jazz delighted in her role as the ward petting dog. She became a firm favourite with patients and nurses and revelled in the attention. She would happily trot along hospital corridors and straight into the ward, cheering the lives of the old and infirm.

When we moved to Spain, in 2002, Jazz took it in her stride and literally jumped for joy at the size of her new garden. With each passing year Jazz became more confident and more popular. If for any reason we went away without her, friends would queue up to look after her.

In 2005 we decided to take a three week break to Lanzarote, over Christmas and New Year. Jazz came along, travelling in the hold as excess baggage. We arrived at Arrecife airport not quite sure of the procedure and hovered around the luggage carousel with all the other passengers. Imagine our surprise when first onto the moving carousel was Jazz. A crescendo of *ahhh,* echoed through the arrivals lounge as Jazz barked her way around the revolving conveyor.

In later life, Jazz overcame major illness and a life threatening accident. Late one evening, on her final outing of the day, she spotted a rabbit and took chase. No longer a young pup, her ageing frame could not take the strain. The vertebrae in her back opened, trapping her spinal cord. She collapsed to the ground paralysed; screaming out in pain. Quickly I gathered her in my arms, ran home and called the emergency vet.

Breaking every speed limit, we arrived at the surgery within minutes. Our urgency saved her life. After spending two weeks motionless, she finally began to recover.

Shortly after her accident, she inexplicably collapsed; the diagnosis, a heart condition. The passing years were taking their toll. Her walks became shorter and less frequent; as a consequence she started to gain a few pounds, or so we thought. So concerned were we over her weight that we decided to speak to the vet. Jazz had been through a lot over the last twelve months but her biggest fight was still to come – cancer.

Her, "few extra pounds" turned out to be a six kilo tumour, the size of a football. Once again she remained strong. For fifteen months she overcame this new medical challenge, much to the surprise of the vet.

'*Increíble, increíble!*' he exclaimed.

Slowly but surely the last grains of sand slipped through her glass. She developed secondary skin cancer. Daily bathing kept her sores clean but they quickly spread. Jazz had given us a lifetime of selfless devotion; the time had come for us to do the same for her.

That final morning broke our hearts. On a warm, sunny autumn day, surrounded by those she loved, Jazz quietly passed away. She had trusted us in life and did the same in death.

Without her, the house felt empty and our lives incomplete. There was no bed to step over or dog to walk around. The house fell silent: I swear Melanie and I spoke more to Jazz than we do to each other.

We couldn't possibly have another: the pain of losing Jazz was too much. We gave everything away, her food, her treats, even her toys. For almost four days we stayed steadfast to our decision.

'You know all those things we were going to do when we didn't have a dog?' I said, on the morning of the fourth day, 'Well I don't want to do them anymore – let's get another.'

We knew that the vet volunteered at a rescue centre; we'd flicked through a folder of *abandonados* when Jazz was being treated.

'I have just the dog for you,' announced the vet. And so she did.

Slawit is our new companion, a beautiful Podenco Galego. Like Jazz it took her a while to settle in, but she has. Our family, and our lives, are once again complete; harmony has been restored.

Giving a rescue dog a loving home will never repay the debt of loyalty they show to you - but it's a great start.

CHICKENS

By Victoria Twead

Also by the Author

Victoria Twead is a New York Times and Wall Street Journal bestselling author. In 2004 she nagged poor, long-suffering Joe into leaving Britain and relocating to a tiny, remote mountain village in the Alpujarras, where they became reluctant chicken farmers and owned the most dangerous cockerel in Spain.

Village life inspired Victoria's first book, *Chickens, Mules and Two Old Fools*, which was quickly followed by more in the Old Fools series, all of which immediately became Amazon bestsellers. www.victoriatwead.com

CHICKENS

By Victoria Twead

Living in the Alpujarra mountains was never dull. One day, Paco, our next door neighbour, pounded on our door with his usual zeal.

"English! Get your coats," he ordered. "We're going to get chickens."

In Paco's Range Rover, Joe and I exchanged furtive glances. Where were we going to keep chickens? The chicken shed in the orchard had been demolished for firewood. How do you look after chickens? Did we really want chickens?

The chicken shop was not what I expected. It displayed every type of cage, hutch, animal feed, mule harness, animal antibiotics and pet paraphernalia imaginable. First we chose a water dispenser and feeder. Then Paco spoke to the assistant who unlocked a long barn. Racks of wire cages were stacked high, each small cage housing about five frightened young chickens. The noise and stench was overpowering. Suddenly the outing had become less of a buying trip and more of a rescue mission. Save some chickens from this ghastly place.

"*¿Cuantos quieren Ustedes?*" asked the assistant. "How many do you want?"

"Two," said Joe.

"Eight," I said.

We stood back and let Paco choose. After all, what did we know about chickens? The assistant reached into the cages and grabbed the chickens that Paco selected. Each chicken was held upside down by its feet and handed over. Paco checked them over, felt their crops expertly, then stuffed them squawking and flapping into the cardboard box provided by the assistant. Six brown chickens and two white.

"They'll never get eight into that tiny box," I muttered to Joe.

But they did. The assistant taped the box shut then produced a wicked looking penknife with which he viciously stabbed the box.

"Air holes," he explained, but I was convinced we would be taking home shredded chicken. They were unharmed, but it reminded me of the stage magic trick where swords are apparently passed through glamorous assistants.

Back in the orchard, Paco pulled his woolly hat off and scratched his head when he saw our chicken shed had gone.

"Qué pasa?" he asked, reproach in his eyes. "What happened to the chicken shed?"

"We burnt it," said Joe. "We used it for firewood."

"Pah!" said Paco and shook his head in disapproval. But he was not a man to be beaten by a little thing like no chicken shed.

Ever resourceful, he dragged over some old doors and leaned them up under the corrugated asbestos roof that was still supported by uprights. There was plenty of chicken wire lying about which he fashioned into a closed-in run secured by bits of wire. He found a stick and fixed it horizontally as a roosting perch.

Time to release the girls. Without ceremony, he emptied the cardboard box and eight chickens slid out to stand stock still like a bizarre waxwork display, frozen on the spot.

"They've never been outside before," I said quietly. "They've never seen the sky. Or grass. Or earth."

Joe nodded. It was a moving moment. Gradually, life flowed back into the eight chickens and they began to explore their new world. Jerky little steps were taken, the ground unfamiliar between their toes. They found the feeder and fed furiously. They took sips of water, tipping their heads back to allow the water to run down their throats. They tasted the grass and picked at tiny specks on the ground. They flapped their wings and stretched - all new luxuries.

"They won't lay eggs for a couple of months," said Paco. "You will need to give them a box to lay in." He left us to it, amused at our rapture.

All work that day was forgotten. We pulled up the old yellow vinyl sofa from the rubbish pile and just sat and watched. It was fascinating. All the chicken cliches we had ever heard suddenly came to life. The 'Top Hen' emerged quickly, one of the white chickens. Bolder than the rest, she pecked anyone who annoyed her and the others treated her with great respect. The 'pecking order' was established. We named her Mala Leche, meaning bad milk, a Spanish insult.

When dusk fell, we were still in the orchard, still fascinated. Instincts kicked in and the girls started craning their necks, looking for the highest place to roost. Mala was the first to fly up to Paco's makeshift perch. The others followed gradually, bickering like schoolgirls about who was going to sit next to whom.

The next morning brought a huge surprise. It's strange how you can wake up and sense something is wrong, something is different. Our bedroom was a cave room dug into the hillside with no windows, but when we woke we knew instinctively that something was awry. We gasped when Joe opened the shutters in the living room to a white and silent world.

The chickens! They'd never even set claw outside before yesterday. We'd plucked them from their indoor security and exposed them to the harshness of a snowstorm. Their shelter was makeshift and inadequate. We were desperately worried.

There was no denying that the mountains looked awesome. Like a monstrous dazzling duvet, the snow blanketed every contour, ironing out all familiar landmarks. But there was no time to enjoy the wonderland. Fat flakes of snow were still falling. We didn't know it then, but this was to be the heaviest snowfall for sixty years. Snow is rare in this part of the world, we lived on the edge of Europe's only desert, for goodness sake. Paco had told us that occasionally a light dusting might fall, but never more.

There was no time to lose. Joe dressed himself warmly in army boots and several jumpers topped by a thick jacket. He opened the front door. Or tried to. The snow had banked to chest height and blocked the door completely. Never mind, we could use the back door. Luckily it faced a different direction and could still be pushed open. Just.

It was bitterly cold. He surveyed the scene outside. "I'm just going outside and may be some time," he said. It wasn't really funny but very apt. Captain Oates would have understood.

The orchard was just a few steps away, the chicken coop a few steps more. But reaching it was tough. The drifts were deep and hid the track. Alonso had used the orchard as a dump and so had we. Obstacles were strewn everywhere. Coils of wire, rubble, the yellow sofa, all smothered and concealed under thick snow. Every footstep was taken warily, like a soldier walking across a minefield.

To Joe's horror, the chicken shelter was one enormous snowdrift. Joe approached with a sinking heart. And then he noticed the drift had a dip in the middle. The ends of the perch disappeared into white, but, locked on the perch, soaking wet and huddled miserably together, were all eight chickens. Their body warmth had melted the snow around them.

How do you dry a chicken? We didn't know. We did the only thing we could think of, which was rub them briskly with old towels. Joe cleared as much snow out of the coop as he could, uncovering their food and water. Luckily, it stopped snowing and a watery sun peeped out, providing much needed warmth.

Chickens are amazingly hardy creatures. They can survive the furnace of an Andalucían summer or winter temperatures below freezing. Even snow. Our chickens, young as they were, were absolutely fine.

By the time the first cuckoo arrived in April, the chickens had settled in well. They had grown in confidence and strutted around the coop happily. We felt they were ready to roam the orchard, so we opened the coop. Mala led the way, followed by Ginger and the No-Name Twins, then the rest. It was more entertaining than T.V.

Chickens are as inquisitive as small children and everything was investigated, even our shoelaces, as we sat on the yellow vinyl sofa watching our flock. When we brought scraps, they hopped on to our knees and ate from our fingers.

Late in the afternoon we decided it was time to lock them up in the coop for the night. Not an easy job. We herded them and succeeded, a few at the time. But as fast as we caught some, others would escape, squirting back through the wire into the orchard. It took half an hour and left us breathless and panting.

"Can't put up with that every night," said Joe.

"Absolutely not!" I said. "But what choice do we have? If we leave them out at night the foxes will have them."

All the next week we went through the same fiasco. Mala was the most cunning. She would wait until we crept up on her, then she'd bolt flapping and squawking across the orchard. We chased chickens round trees, over old furniture, across piles of rubble ... they ran everywhere except back into the coop.

"Quick! The No-Name Twins are coming your way!" yelled Joe. I hurled myself at the nearest Twin and succeeded in grabbing one small tail feather and a mouthful of grit.

"I've got one!" shouted Joe, triumphantly carrying a protesting, squawking Blanca over to the coop. It was inevitable that an old coil of wire would trip him up. Blanca struggled free and bolted to the far side of the orchard.

"Well, the foxes can bloody well eat you! I don't care!" said Joe to all chickens in general. However, in spite of severe sense of humour loss, we persevered and every last chicken was eventually caught and shut in the coop.

One memorable night we were late. The sun had already dipped behind the mountain and the street-lights had flickered into life. Fully prepared to repeat our usual frenzied chase, we looked for the chickens. There was no sign of a single chicken in the whole orchard.

"Where are they?" said Joe, peering into the twilight gloom.

"The fox has had them," I said, guilt washing over me in painful waves.

The sky was turning inky, pierced with pinpoints of starlight. The village rooftops were mere silhouettes and the trees and bushes blurred shapes. The unearthly bark of a fox ricocheted around the valley.

A chicken coughed and we swung round. In the coop, on the perch, like a row of naughty schoolgirls, sat eight chickens, six brown and two white. The saying 'chickens coming home to roost' became evident. And so it was, as soon as the sun set, the girls would put themselves to bed. No fuss, no chasing. Another chicken cliche nailed.

I never dreamed that chickens were interesting, but I was wrong. Each individual developed her own personality, comical to the extreme. Fraidy was the coward of the bunch, setting off alarm calls if a beetle crossed her path. Shawly (so named because of her darker head and shoulders) was the kleptomaniac. Slowly, stealthily, she would sneak up behind the others and launch a surprise raid, whipping juicy morsels from under their beaks. Then she would dash away like an Oxford Street mugger and gobble her spoils in a hidden corner. Ginger was the boldest and most sociable, the first to greet us at the gate, the one to stay and chat if we sat on the sofa.

We were utterly hooked, these silly birds so delighted us with their funny ways. For example, when we came to the orchard empty handed, we were ignored, except, of course, by Ginger who met us at the gate and told us all her news at great length.

However, if we were carrying the blue plastic treat box containing kitchen scraps, their welcome was very different. Eight chickens charged to the gate, some flying like feathered bricks, some running, heads down, legs pumping like pistons. They would arrive in a heap, disentangle themselves and press against the fence. The excitement was intense. Necks became elongated as they craned up, desperate to see what the treats box contained. They wound round our feet, tripping us up. So we'd throw a few scraps as far as possible and they'd all thunder to the spot like rugby players. If we threw more in a different direction, they'd all abandon the first scraps and career over to the latest offerings. Another rugby scrum, until all scraps were exhausted. If the scraps contained spaghetti, two chickens might grab either end of a strand. They would suck in their end until they finished up eyeball to eyeball - unless Shawly sneaked in and stole the middle section.

We grew ridiculously fond of our girls. Sometimes we talked about the horrible chicken shop and I suppose it was only a matter of time before we found ourselves there again.

This time, the cages contained some young black chickens and some ravishing grey and speckled ones. As before, the stench and noise was overpowering. It was even more distressing to see the unfortunate chickens packed together in tiny cages now that we understood chicken behaviour so much better.

"*¿Cuantos quieren Ustedes?*" asked the assistant. "How many do you want?"

"Two," said Joe.

"Eight," I said.

We couldn't wait to get them home. In the jeep, we told them all about their new home and how they would be able to scratch in the dirt and spread their wings. We told them all about the chickens already there. We warned them about Shawly stealing their food, and told them to take no notice of Mala and her bossy ways. They were quiet in their box so we assumed they were listening carefully to our advice.

In the orchard, the older chickens were consumed with curiosity. They circled the cardboard box, chattering amongst themselves.

"We've brought you some new friends," said Joe, gently upending the box. The new girls slid out, blinking in the sudden light. We were about to learn a huge lesson in chicken politics.

Attack! With squawks of rage, the original girls set about the newcomers. The air turned thick with chicken swear words and insults. The little ones shrieked with terror and cowered as the big girls pounced. Beaks stabbed, feathers were wrenched and became airborne before drifting back to ground.

81

It was World War 3, and then some. The new kids in the flock fled, scattered to all corners of the orchard. Total disaster. Our visions of one big happy chicken family sadly dissolved.

The original eight, now known collectively as 'The Mafia', were relentless. Even gentle Ginger revealed an alter ego we had never suspected. The new girls hid under bushes and behind trees because as soon as they were spotted by the Mafia, they were hammered. Doing great impressions of Road Runner, they fled to escape from their bullies. In Britain, the Mafia would all have been served Antisocial Behaviour Orders.

We were at a complete loss. The new girls were uncatchable, scattered to all points of the compass.

I wondered if the Internet might help, and typed in 'introducing new chickens to an existing flock'. The results were varied.

The first advice page adopted the 'No Nonsense' approach, as follows:

Introducing New Hens to the Flock

Where new birds are introduced to an existing flock, there are always problems because the natural pecking order is disrupted. A hen spotting a newcomer will utter a single warning croak that alerts the rest of the flock. It then becomes fair game to peck at and chase away the stranger.

If it is absolutely necessary to introduce new birds to an existing flock they should be penned in a temporary area next to the run so that they can be seen but not harmed.

Birds can also be beak-trimmed so that they are less able to do damage to each other. The procedure is to trim the pointed tip of the upper mandible of the beak.

Once the birds are taking each other for granted, they can be amalgamated, but a careful watch needs to be kept for potential problems.

Well, it was much too late to erect a separate pen and introduce the new ones slowly. And there was no way we were going to catch the Mafia and trim their beaks. Unthinkable. I sighed and pulled up another poultry advice page.

This one was … well, frankly, ridiculous.

How to introduce new chickens to an existing flock

Allow the new bird to roam around a bit in your kitchen (where the inevitable poop won't be too difficult to clean up) or bathroom while you croon SOFTLY to it and feed it little bits of cheese, lunchmeat, diced grapes, raw corn, etc. Sit down on the floor so you aren't towering over it and give it a good 20 minutes to get to know you, and realize what a TERRIFIC person you are. Pick it up and pet it, talking softly and cooing to it all the while. Keep your voice GENTLE, soothing and quiet. Watch your birds' eyes--you may see the pupil expanding and contracting rapidly. This signals excitement, in a GOOD way, for birds. It means that they REALLY like what you are doing to them. Continue to coo at it and praise it for the good little chicken it is. Chickens LOVE to be talked to in a loving tone.

Pick it up and take it into the yard during the day. Hold it tucked under your arm and call your flock. Continue to hold and PET the new bird as you talk to the flock and walk around the yard a bit, showing the new bird around. Walk in and out of the coop. View the nest boxes. Point out the food and water dishes. Give 'em the two dollar tour.

When everyone is ready, go ahead and put the new bird down slowly and stand next to it. Warn them off with a firm, "NOOO--!" and take a step towards them if need be. You may need to chase off aggressors a bit.

YOU are the TOP HEN! Remember, and what YOU say, GOES! Praise GOOD behavior. After a while, your flock WILL remember they have better things to do, lose interest and wander away. After that it's safe to go back inside the house, leaving the new bird to its own devices.

Oh, please! Our Spanish neighbours already thought we were insane, sitting on the yellow sofa gazing at our flock, letting them hop onto our laps, talking to them. Even if we could catch the newcomers, taking eight chickens, putting them into the bathroom and whispering sweet nothings into their ears was bordering on complete lunacy.

When night fell, the Mafia went to bed and the little ones regrouped. They found the grain feeder and water and gorged themselves while the coast was clear. Finally, they too went to bed, on the floor under the Mafia's perch. It was an uneasy truce.

For the next couple of weeks work on the house suffered. The punch-ups were so severe that we felt obliged to go into the orchard on 'playground duty'. At least that way we could break up some of the fights. But I suppose we were lucky as the orchard was big and had plenty of hiding places. No chicken was ever badly wounded. And as the little ones grew in size and confidence the confrontations dwindled.

Weeks drifted by and we had still not seen an egg. The Internet advised us to provide a dark, quiet box and suggested we place some golf balls inside to give the chickens the right idea. Joe found an old discarded wooden trunk and cut an entrance in the front. The girls explored it thoroughly but no eggs were forthcoming. Every day we lifted the lid of the trunk hopefully and every day we were disappointed. Perhaps they were hiding their eggs around the orchard?

One day we entered the orchard, with treat box, and were mobbed as usual. All seemed fine except that Ginger was behaving in a very strange fashion. She was agitated, nervous, obviously troubled by something. We sat down on the sofa, and Ginger hopped onto Joe's lap and buried her head under his arm. Then she tried to get herself inside his jacket, it was most peculiar.

"Do you think she's ill?" I asked.

"I think she might want to lay an egg," Joe said. He carried her tenderly over to the wooden trunk and popped her in, blocking off the exit. She scrabbled about at first, then went completely quiet. Half an hour ticked past, then the scrabblings started again.

"I'll let her out," said Joe, and unblocked the entrance hole of the trunk.

Ginger came out, blinked and stood still. Then she stretched herself very tall, pointed her beak to the sky, and sang. Well, perhaps not everybody would call it 'singing', chickens not being the most tuneful of creatures. But it was a song of sorts, a 'bok bok bok bok BOKKKKKKK!' sort of song which later became very familiar to us. It was the triumphant Egg Song.

And sure enough, snug in the straw, still warm, so precious, was a perfect little egg.

The Egg Song was heard increasingly as they all started laying. It became a daily pleasure to lift the lid of the trunk and reveal that clutch of perfect eggs, like finding treasure in a pirate's chest.

The trouble was, we hadn't done our sums. A quick session with the calculator revealed that sixteen chickens, laying one egg each per day, lay a total of one hundred and twelve eggs a week. That's four hundred and forty eggs a month. Let's be fair, and allow the chickens a day off every few days. That still amounts to about four hundred eggs a month. An awesome amount of eggs.

Joe took a dozen eggs with him to Marcia's shop to give away. It was the weekend and the bread van happened to be there surrounded by village ladies.

"Would anyone like some eggs?" he asked. He was almost trampled in the rush. The eggs were snatched out of his hands, and orders were placed for more. One of the Smart Ladies advised Joe to charge 70 cents for half a dozen in future, and so our unplanned business was born.

Joe put up a ship's bell outside our garden gate and our customers rang it constantly. But selling eggs was a mixed blessing. It caused problems we had not envisaged. The ship's bell would clang at all hours of the day, a constant interruption. Many a barrow of plaster or cement was ruined, abandoned while we served and chatted with an egg customer. Sometimes the bell would ring at eleven o'clock at night. Joe was not pleased.

And woe betide if I had no eggs left. "But it's for the children!" the lady would wail as though I was a hard-hearted witch to deprive them.

Sometimes the egg sales even caused fights outside our gate when two customers arrived at the same time. I could hear their conversation from inside.

"Oh, Maria! How are you?"

"Not bad, not bad. And you?"

"Fine, I'm just getting my eggs from the English."

"Yes, me too. I need them for a cake."

"I need them for the children."

"Well, I was here first. The English know I always come on Sunday mornings."

"No, Maria. I already told the English I was baking a cake today."

The voices would be growing in volume and I'd nervously check our egg supplies. Then I'd go down and open the gate and let them both in. Their faces would be wreathed in smiles belying the fact that they'd nearly come to blows in the street. We'd all agree that the eggs were very fresh and tasty. If there were enough eggs, the purchases would be made and the ladies would leave triumphantly. If not, I would have to send Joe to the orchard to see if there were any more while the ladies sat glowering at each other and me. Sometimes the chickens simply could not lay fast enough, which resulted in the two ladies not speaking to each other, or me.

Often, the Egg Ladies would give me instructions. "I need eggs next weekend. Keep them for me, please. Don't sell them to that Maria."

The next lady would arrive. "Keep a dozen for me next Saturday, I've got family staying. Don't sell them to that Teresa."

Joe once suggested (only half jokingly) that we buy extra eggs from the supermarket to make up the shortfall. That way we wouldn't upset any of our Egg Ladies. And perhaps we could have eggs, too, as during that period we rarely tasted an egg ourselves.

Dogs... Smarter Than The Average Bear

By David Bull

Dogs... Smarter Than The Average Bear

By David Bull

Why does she have to do it? And always in front of guests... it drives me mad but come what may, no matter what time of day or night, never mind that she's just been for a long walk to do all the necessaries and smell as many turds as is possible in thirty minutes (there's probably a website dedicated to it somewhere...) she has to do it in front of you. Many a time I've had 'company' and just as the DVD is getting going and the wine is warming the bodies and loosening the tongues. Just as the candles are burning down and you've made 'that' move and snuggled up a tad closer....along comes Megan my mongrel, across the front of the TV, dragging her backside along the rug, with the most satisfied of grins on her face. Having not embarrassed me enough at this point she will then turn around and sniff along her recent route whilst enthusiastically wagging her tail. Man's best friend.... MY arse....

Got the dog inoculated for Rabies this month, Rabies? My dog? What a waste of money that was – she's always running around the house with wild staring eyes and foaming at the mouth, a little dose of Rabies would probably go unnoticed and I seriously challenge the idea of Rabies taking hold in a country like Spain anyway. I mean, can you imagine? The disease reaches the Spanish border with packs of wild dogs roaming and fighting and chasing everything that crosses their path. They then reach the 'checkpoint' and pass on the disease to the resident Spanish strays who have just had an afternoon's siesta and are preparing to wind down for the evening with a late meal in the usual alleyway followed by a good night's rest curled up with friends. Now I could be wrong about this but I can see the Spanish mutts opening one eye, to witness their French cousins snarling and frothing, as they themselves lay

87

basking in the sun and rejecting the Rabies route as far too energetic. Have you seen any Rabid dogs around here lately? I didn't think so... you see the theory holds up and goes one step further, you see, give it a few years and 'Yuppie Flu' may well make it to the Iberian peninsular and I can see it now, a pack of Spanish dogs cocking their heads to one side as news of the lethargic disease reaches them and their thoughts turning to: 'now THAT'S a disease...'Got the dog inoculated for Rabies this month, Rabies? My dog? What a waste of money that was – she's always running around the house with wild staring eyes and foaming at the mouth, a little dose of Rabies would probably go unnoticed and I seriously challenge the idea of Rabies taking hold in a country like Spain anyway. I mean, can you imagine? The disease reaches the Spanish border with packs of wild dogs roaming and fighting and chasing everything that crosses their path. They then reach the 'checkpoint' and pass on the disease to the resident Spanish strays who have just had an afternoon's siesta and are preparing to wind down for the evening with a late meal in the usual alleyway followed by a good night's rest curled up with friends. Now I could be wrong about this but I can see the Spanish mutts opening one eye, to witness their French cousins snarling and frothing, as they themselves lay basking in the sun and rejecting the Rabies route as far too energetic. Have you seen any Rabid dogs around here lately? I didn't think so... you see the theory holds up and goes one step further, you see, give it a few years and 'Yuppie Flu' may well make it to the Iberian peninsular and I can see it now, a pack of Spanish dogs cocking their heads to one side as news of the lethargic disease reaches them and their thoughts turning to: 'now THAT'S a disease...'

Jonathan Twit

By Jonathan Fogell

Jonathan Twit

By Jonathan Fogell

Dot and Jonathan were fifty somethings whose sons had all flown the nest. They gave up their secure well paid jobs in the UK to take on the simple task of running a bar in Orgiva. They had a wonderful time but, as their first day's experiences showed, it was not trouble free by any means.

The laughing clown outside the Fun House on Blackpool Pleasure Beach always annoyed rather than amused me. His laugh seemed so insincere. As I awoke that morning May 1st 2003, I imagined everyone I met having a laugh like that, and I was the source of amusement. "Look at him", they would shout, "the old fool. Wouldn't you have thought he'd know better at his age". I imagined a world infinitely crueller in its judgements of me and much more ready to point an accusing finger. All social niceties had disappeared and everyone jumped to the most damning of conclusions. The problem was of course I didn't have a plausible excuse for my behaviour.

Many people say that if you have a big problem you should sleep on it. I had slept on it, well I had slept a little. I went to bed a little bit anxious and woke up, having rehearsed both when awake and in my sleep, every possible disastrous scenario. I rose from my bed feeling wretched.

I remembered a John Glashan cartoon. A solitary figure stood alone in the centre of the drawing. In every direction, there were thousands of people running away from him. Showing the urgency of their flight, their arms were flayed, hair streamed, torsos leant determinedly forward like Usain Bolt just out of the starting blocks. The subject in the centre with shoulders down and dejected expression was saying "I've got problems". Well, now I had problems.

I attempted a little personal reality orientation. If I was somebody else hearing about me with all that had been done in the last few days and weeks, and I knew they were feeling this crushing self-doubt what would I say about them? "Well-done mate I admire you for having a go. Life is not a rehearsal you have to go out and make it interesting or, before you know it, it will have passed you by". Then my inner voice would kick in and say, "crap! If what you are doing is so good, how come nobody else is doing it?"

Such thoughts were going through my mind I was preparing to set off my first day as the owner of Casa Santiago in Orgiva. "How do you feel?" said Dot as I sat ponderously on the end of the bed "Like shite", I replied as I headed off to make a cup of tea. As I made my way between boxes, I noticed that Pippa our Border Collie was lying on our son Ashley's bed. "Get down" I snapped and that seemed reassuringly normal for me.

I took a bath and then dressed in the clothes bought especially for working in the bar: smart tee shirt and thin cotton long black trousers. We had signed contracts with Jose on our arrival the previous day. I had then agreed to meet Jose at the bar at eight the next morning. I was there at exactly eight o'clock to start my new life, but I was on my own. I sat on the green plastic seats outside the bar and looked up the main street of Orgiva. The church with its twin towers watched over the town and I could see each of the shops, bars and banks coming to life. Padre Jose arrived at about eight-fifteen and Jose at eight-twenty.

Both Jose's greeted me warmly and then watched as I disconnected the alarm and unlocked the front doors. The little bar strongly smelled of woodsmoke. It wasn't just the after-effects of cigarettes and cigars mingling with the beer and spilt wine to produce that characteristic acrid morning odour present in all bars. This was more like the smell on one's clothes when one had been standing close to a bonfire. Jose Padre headed for the bar and started making everyone a cup of coffee. Jose spoke rapidly in an impenetrable Andalucían Spanish. He was, however, incredibly patient with me.

Jose showed me each of the electrical switches and pointed out what they operated. He impressed upon me that switch five, out of eighteen, had to be left on all night. This worked the alarm, water in the coffee machine and the freezers to continue to keep the provisions cold. The light in the ladies toilets was on the same circuit and so had to be turned off each night, because electricidad cost mucho dinero. Mucho dinero, was one of the phrases I learnt quickly from Jose. Spending it was to be avoided at all costs. Poco dinero was better to spend but a disaster to earn. I also learnt mejor (better) very quickly as something to aim for. As for the rest of the Andalucian brand of Spanish, that would have to wait.

I was instructed with practical demonstrations of each necessary task and the phrase 'es mejor asi' (its better this way). The first job was to clean the chairs on the terrace. Initially, I thought this to be a little unnecessary, but a glance up the street revealed every bar with somebody outside wiping down the chairs. Orgiva was a very dusty place. Inside or out, any item motionless for only a matter of minutes would be covered with a fine layer of dust. If it rained, the entire area was often covered with a thin layer of red Sahara sand. The static electricity created by bums and thighs rubbing against plastic helped the dust to adhere to the chairs. If it had rained in the night, which thankfully was seldom, the chairs and tables looked filthy. Many of our customers wore light coloured or white clothing and would be repelled by the sight of dirty plastic chairs. So the job had to be done every day.

It was in showing me this that Jose revealed one important omission in the bar. There was no hot water. At least at this time in the morning there was none. The chairs and tables were washed down with spray cleaner and cold water rinse. In England this would have been a rotten job but here in the warmth of the Spanish morning it was quite pleasant. It also gave me the opportunity to see folks passing by to bid them good morning and to make the statement Casa Santiago is here to serve you. For all those reasons, strange though it may seem, I liked washing the chairs and table in the morning.

Next was learning how to work the coffee machine. This was going to be more complicated than I had first imagined. , I quickly mastered simple tasks like grinding the coffee, measuring a dose, putting the filter on the machine and pressing the right buttons. More complicated was learning the range of different cups of coffee solo, con leche, cortado, mancharda, cortado con muy poco leche, café heilo. Translating what the customer had asked for into amounts of coffee and milk was a total confusion to me. Jose watched over the first dozen or so cups I served but then left me to it, unless I called for help. The first customer I served floored everyone by asking for two Café Lattes in a broad Dutch accent. It took a few seconds for me to realise he was asking for milky coffees and that was then translated into café con leches for Jose and then my instruction began. We had a steady stream of customers coming in for coffee and so by the time Ashley arrived mid morning, I was looking quite proficient and he was impressed.

Dot had arrived at nine o'clock and Adrianna the cook arrived at nine-thirty. They were in the kitchen working out how to communicate with each other and Adrianna was showing Dot by demonstration how the different tapas were prepared. The first customer came in for a beer at about eleven o'clock. Jose served the beer and then beckoned me to watch as he carved the Jamon. The long slender knife was sharpened with a few slashes on the sharpening iron. He took hold of the Jamon, which was resting on its stand on the back shelf of the bar. He leant forward so that the centre of gravity could counter the cutting motions with the knife against the flesh of the jamon. Then with swift deliberate and assertive strokes he cut five slices each about two centimetres wide, ten centimetres long and about a millimetre thick. He placed jamon over the top of four breadsticks and placed them in front of the customer who has just ordered a Caña 25 mls of beer. The customer looked away as the tapa was placed in front of him and the as Jose walked away the recipient looked carefully at his gift and picked a piece of jamon up and started eating it. Jose looked at me and said Tapa.

It was the custom in Casa Santiago to serve hot tapas between eleven thirty and three thirty. At all other times, Jose gave a tapa of cold meat, chorizo, paté or cheese. The cooked tapas for this particular day were:

Primera   Albondiga, (a meatball served in a tomato sauce),

Segunda   Migas (savoury semolina served with either a small piece of sausage or black pudding),

Tercera   Aasedores (stew prepared with a range of offal normally reserved for dog meat in England),

Cuarto   Sangre, (congealed chickens' blood cooked with tomato and onion) and

Cincuenta   Bacalao,(salt cod battered and then served in a tomato sauce).

Each of these were prepared in a medium sized saucepan and were numbered so that Jose, or anybody else serving behind the bar, could snap out the number for speed of working.

Customers arrived thick and fast by eleven thirty. Every few minutes Jose would introduce me to somebody new. After handshakes and bidding me 'beuna suerte' they would join their group. All of the people Jose introduced me to were Spanish. Many of them were other bar owners who had come in to introduce themselves and to wish me luck. The clientele appeared to be about eighty per-cent Spanish fifteen percent English and five percent other Europeans.

93

There was one old man who sat in the corner of the bar. He ordered a Rosado and I mistakenly replied Rosada. He corrected me and the pointed elaborately to the half full bottle of Rose wine stood on the bar. I poured him a drink and then went about my business. He had waited for about ten seconds before he shouted Tapa. Jose sprang to action, popped behind the curtain that separated the bar from the kitchen and emerged with a small plate of migas with a longoniza (spicy sausage) and a small slice of fried aubergine on it. He placed the plate in front of the old man and then took a spoon and placed this on the little mound of food. The old man grunted and then picked up the spoon and started eating.

Jose beckoned me behind the curtain and then quietly told me using words and gestures that every time a client orders a wine or a beer they should be given a tapa. I was surprised at this. Some, in fact almost anybody you asked, would say at this point that we had not done our research properly. I could hear that little man from the pleasure beach roaring with laughter and all around were joining in with him. I did not have time to dwell on that as drink after drink was ordered. Tapas were going backwards and forwards along the bar. The room was full of cigarette smoke and money did not change hands except when a customer was leaving and they said, 'Cuanto es?' (how much?). Jose would immediately ask them for a figure. I did not work out ever whether Jose asked them for an approximation of what it came to, erring on the low side for the Spanish, and the high side for the English and other groups. I suspect that he erred on the next to nothing side for his many mates that came in, but perhaps I am too harsh on him. I quickly learned that I had to keep notes behind the bar of what different groups had taken so that I could calculate their bill. This was the source of much amusement for many of the locals.

Once there were a few people in the bar the activity was constant. Whenever there was a lull in orders, it was time to fill the fridges with bottles of beer or other soft drinks, clean up or replenish the bottles on the bar with draught wine from the bodega. At one point when there were only two or three customers in the bar. I took the brush out to clear some of the ankle deep debris that had been dropped by the customers. There were used serviettes, spent cigarette packets, discarded unsuccessful lottery tickets, score sheets from the domino players who occupied a table on the terrace and hundreds if not thousands of cigarette butts. The ashtrays spread liberally about the bar had one or two butts in each but the floor was covered in them.

Jose told me it was regarded as bad manners for the barmen to sweep up when the customers were still there. More importantly if they saw you sweeping up, they might assume you were closing resulting in poco dinero which was a bad thing. Most importantly here a dirty bar denoted a well-used bar and therefore people would be attracted to it. I found it curious that people would be attracted to come and eat and drink in a place that was filthy but I was assured that was correct.

After four Rosados and tapas, the old chap at the side of the bar looked up from his paper as I passed and said in a gravel voice "Jonathan Twit". I wondered what I had done to deserve that. Was it because I had called his Rosado, Rosada? Was it because I had forgotten his tapa not once but twice. Was it because I had to ask everyone to repeat what they wanted and even then it required Jose to show me where things were. "Jonathan Twit" he shouted, the words growling out through phlegm and gravel again, and his thick, pungent cigarette in his hand. Was it because he knew how I felt and what a stupid bastard I had been to think that I could come to a foreign land and do a job I knew next to nothing about? Was he the man from the pleasure beach and would he suddenly start to laugh. Would all the rest of the people in the bar turn and look at him and then at me, Jonathan Twit, and start to laugh as well. It would not surprise me because I deserved it. After the third booming Jonathan Twit, I decided to confront this particular demon.

I recalled reading somewhere that when dealing with important matters the Spanish tend to get very close to their co-respondent and talk conspiratorially. Keeping "la distancia" was a sign of disrespect. That was what I had to do. I walked up the bar towards the old man. He smiled as I approached and said in a softer more welcoming tone "Jonathan Twit". I had rehearsed in my mind several times what I was going to say. "por qué Jonathan Twit?" I said as if to talk confidentially to a best friend. (Why Jonathan Twit?) "Gulliver Travel" he replied. It was like having a boil lanced. "Si Jonathan Swift escritor muy buenot. He smiled and said Jonathan Twit and then went back to reading his paper.

By four o'clock in the afternoon, we had quietened down and so had the town. We had served one meal during this rather frenetic lunchtime. It consisted of a starter of onion soup. Adrianna prepared this by placing the terracotta bowl over the full gas and then placing in ham stock from the fridge, sliced onion, cooked bread and cheese salt and pepper. It was delicious but somewhat hazardous as a result of the bowl that was crucible hot as we served it. I warned the customer to be extremely careful with the bowl. This was followed by Habas con jamon, a local delicacy consisted of onions garlic and Jamon fried in lashings of olive oil. To this was added a plateful of cooked broad beans. It was all simmered for a while and then served with a sprig of mint and half a stick of bread. It was swimming in olive oil and looked most unappetizing but the customer appeared to enjoy it immensely.

At four in the afternoon, I suggested that Dot went home and return at six. "Why don't you close the bar and come home for a rest", Dot enquired. "No, for today I need to see how it is done by Jose's standards. What I did not realise was that today, I could not see it by Jose's normal pattern because it was not a normal day. All of the workers in the town had the day off except those working in bars. The pattern of business was therefore totally different. Also, Jose was determined to impress me. The matador in him was determined to show that real men work like slaves. I did agree with Jose that if Padre Jose could hold the fort for an hour or so we could each take a short break before the evening session. If the day had been anything to go by it would be a busy evening.

I walked away from the bar and noticed the sweet smell of the clean fresh air. The sun hurt my eyes after the dim lights of Casa Santiago. Electriciy costing mucha dinero was a bad thing. Jose had therefore installed energy saving lights throughout the bar. These differed from ordinary lights in two ways, they did not cost much and two they didn't light much. It was a bar with subtle, subdued lighting to diners and drinkers. It was a dingy little bar to passers by and those of us who had to work in there. When I got back to the flat Dot was waiting and eager for a debrief on the days unusual set of experiences. I was ready to flop.

"What is all that Tapa thing about? Dot asked.

I don't know.

Did you know we were supposed to give a tapa out with every single drink?

No, I did not.

Well, we should have researched this thing Jon. Adrianna and I have worked all morning and we have only sold one thing. Everything else has been given away.

I know. I don't know how we can deal with it. It's not as though they sit and wait patiently. "Tapa" they shout, "Tapa" and expect it to be put in front of them without a word of thanks or even acknowledgement that you have given them something.

Do you want a drink? said Ashley.

Oh wonderful, pour a nice cold beer for me will you mate;

When Ashley placed the beer in front of me I turned to him with a look of indignation on my face and I shouted "Tapa!"

He said, "get it yourself Jonathan Twit", and we all chuckled.

Lead For Gold

By Lizzie Wynn

Lead For Gold

By Lizzie Wynn

His dreamlike state became consciousness, in a city called Winnipeg. He spent his days blissfully suckling from his huge mother; dozing and frolicking with his siblings. Satisfying, to be sure, though there was something missing. He felt a longing for a greater purpose and wanted to satisfy more than his instinctive urges for survival. There was something about the humans that drove him to strive for their reassuring tones and interesting expressions. Their attention was like gold to him, his amber nectar. They held a secret to his yearnings.

As he grew from the size of a mouse to the size of a rat, he experimented with looks and noises to create different reactions in the humans, to find what delighted them most. They were easy to please however, so the task was not difficult. He heard the words, Jack Russell, frequently, so presumed that was his name. He began to feel fearless and huge and could never resist chasing a good scent.

He was beginning to expect that his whole life would be lived out there with his family, playing and feeding, when an odd sounding fellow came to his door, this fellow meant business. His name was Seamus and he had come from a faraway place called Ireland, but lived in Canada now. He had a presence that was hard to define. As he studied the pups intensely and picked them up, examining them carefully, a tiny smile appeared at the corner of his mouth. Seamus had waited a long time to find dogs like these and he wasn't about to choose one quickly. He had an ambition. The mother growled menacingly but this only put a gleam in Seamus' eye. He appreciated her animosity.

He soon found himself wrapped in a blanket and shoved into a strange smelling box with a satisfying chewy toy inside. As he was carried about, the smells entering the vents from outside lifted him to a new realm of pleasure, whilst the contrast of the temperature and the noise, left him chilled and nervous. He ached for his familiar world, with the warmth of his family, but also felt thrilled by the change. Changes indeed were ahead as his unsettling journey led to sheer terror. He was lifted into the belly of a metal bird and all the light was extinguished. Deafening noises followed and his stomach lurched.

After an immeasurable, miserable time, he emerged into the blinding light feeling wretched. He was chilled to the bone within moments and feared for his life. Diving under the blanket, he was determined not to come out until he felt brave again. A short time later though after a ride in a comfy, warm box on wheels, he was picked up by Seamus and carried out with his blanket into a place that felt far more appropriate to his needs.

***

As the weeks passed by, Mr Finnegan acquired his name, a collar, more chew toys, a soft bed in a warm wooden house and a deep love for his three new people. Seamus was kind and extremely firm, but his wife and son became his loving playmates. He was in a place called Dawson City and he didn't like the cold of it. It made him shiver in fear, but torn between a warm bed and a beckoning voice, the human always triumphed. With their call came exciting adventures in delicious smelling woods and streets. They dressed him in a smart, stiff jacket that was awful to wear, but it made him feel as if he would not perish whilst out for a stroll. Boots were next as the temperature dropped frightening and the ground turned icy and white and stayed that way.

Feeling that the pleasure he was experiencing, with his humans, could not be equalled or bettered anywhere, he grew into an adult dog feeling deeply contented, yet not knowing what joy still awaited him. He had an enviable gait, the happiest walk in the world, his people said.

It was early morning when he watched, incredulously, as his people left the house one day without him. Feeling desolate, he took solace in his comforting bed, praying they wouldn't leave him for long. The bed was lovely, but laps were so much better. It was a long wait, dark when he heard his people pull into the driveway. Finally. Such a frenzy of delight engulfed him that he couldn't make enough noise or stop jumping high in the air, when all at once a familiar and delicious scent hit his delicate nostrils. It was like the smell of his mother, yet more exciting. He would have been stopped in mid jump if gravity hadn't been around. As he struggled onto his paws again, a box was set on the floor containing that enticing smell. An exhausted looking female, Jack Russell terrier lifted her head and looked back at him curiously She seemed to smile as her head sank back onto her blanket.

Mr Finnegan and his new friend, Siobhan, got along brilliantly. He introduced her to her new home, showed her the walks and they curled up together to sleep. Life indeed got better, Mr Finnegan found new feelings he didn't know existed. Mr Finnegan had found love.

One morning, Siobhan stayed home, preferring not to walk out with him. In disbelief, Mr Finnegan went for the usual romp in the snow and found the scent of a fox. Caught up in the chase, he stayed out far longer than normal and arrived home tired and happy, not knowing the changes that awaited him. He sought out Siobhan, following a strange, scent that he recognised that engulfed the whole house. All he could do was stand still and blink when he found Siobhan. She had somehow divided herself into smaller pieces that were wriggling around her limp form. As he realised the truth, a sense of pride overcame him and his little chest swelled. He licked her warm lovely face and surveyed his seven new sons and daughters.

Mr Finnegan observed his Seamus working on an odd contraption that summer, taking his time with the details, but he didn't see it being used once it seemed to be finished. What he did witness though was his pups thriving, maturing and become strong and nimble. Outings were noisy and lively with long chases after squirrels, ravens and anything that moved really. They all felt so good and their tiny muscles hardened on their sleek bodies.

The autumn chill came too soon and the first snow began to fall. More jackets and boots appeared and preparations for outings took forever. The walks seemed to be longer each day however, much to the dogs delight. Seamus lit the fire in his garden workshop and spent long hours out there when he wasn't walking the dogs. Eventually he dragged his offering out into the cold and sat on it. He seemed to think it was enormous fun, sliding it around on the gently sloping driveway. It was long, light and sleek, with space for two humans to sit. Further adjustments were made then Mr Finnegan was summoned.

His harness was snug, the ropes strong. Urged to walk forward Mr Finnegan found he could move the sled easily and it felt good indeed to pull. Seamus was utterly delighted and whooped in encouragement. Mr Finnegan's heart thudded with excitement. They practiced hard and well. The next step however was a disaster, with all the terrier family involved. Siobhan could not be heard by the excited pups. All harnessed in together they dragged the sled in every way but forward whilst Seamus cursed them. Mr Finnegan growled angrily at them and pounced on the loudest. Silence. Siobhan quietly instructed them to follow their father and meekly they obeyed. Poetry in motion, it worked like a dream. Steadily, they worked together, the velocity increased, their forces entwined. Seamus mounted the sled and they careered down the avenue, unstoppable. Seamus yelled out in glee, so proud of his fantastic little dogs and their combined muscle power. Nine Jack Russell's hitched to the sled, his crazy dream, at last a reality. Mr Finnegan's happiness could not be equalled as he breathed in the freezing air and mustered all his energy. He was bursting with pride, enjoying his new found gold. Mr Finnegan, the lead dog. Joy, oh joy!

Lola's Story

By Arpy Shively

Arpy and her partner Fred arrived in Lanjarón in 2003 with their bearded collie Macduff, ex-Yorkshire, ex-Washington DC. Lola arrived in 2006; they fostered Bonnie and Max in Orgiva from 2009 to 2012; these days a Westie/Maltese rescue, Eddie, shares their city-centre apartment in Málaga.

Lola's Story

By Arpy Shively

The first time I saw the pretty black and white spaniel, on a fine morning in May 2006, she was lying in the middle of the Plaza in Órgiva, quietly starving, while kids played football and elderly neighbours chatted around her. I walked quickly past, though my heart ached and I was angry that people were so indifferent. But we had a dog, I was going to London later that week, I couldn't get involved.

An hour later, shopping done and coffee drunk but still sad, I was heading down the high street towards my car at the other end of town. I looked down and there was this black and white bag of bones, hobbling alongside. As soon as I spoke to her, she rolled over on her back as if to play.

I didn't even think, just took my scarf off and tied it round her neck. She was crawling with ticks and very weak. One paw was swollen and sore, and she had a huge red lump distorting one eyelid. I wrapped her in my anorak. A group of elderly Brits were walking past and stopped to look. I remember one man was crying. He thanked me for rescuing her. I asked a passer-by to carry her to my car and we put her in the well. I called my friend Annie and asked her to come with me to the vet, so the little dog could be put to sleep and out of pain.

I stopped at home to show my husband and explain about the vet. "Poor little thing," he said, "I wonder if she can eat anything?" He brought out a few slices of ham and some water. She snatched at the ham, and I began to see possibilities.

"What's her name?" asked the vet.

"What's your name?" I asked the vet.

"Lola."

So Lola it was. Lola was between four and five years old and severely undernourished. She had a grass spear in her paw, which had become infected, a congenital eye defect, a plague of ticks and possible leishmania. They kept her in overnight, put her on a drip and the tests came back negative – miraculously she didn't have the dreaded disease. Once they had spayed her and operated on her eye and her paw, we could take her home. Lola soon became the princess in the kitchen, living room, bedroom and our hearts.

When we left the country for a small city apartment where pets weren't allowed, we paid friends to care for her and she stayed in the countryside she loved.

When you rescue a dog, from the street or from a shelter, your efforts are lovingly repaid every single day, every hour, every time you see them happy, well fed and safe. Every dog should be a loved dog, but until then, go out and find one and make it part of your forever family. You'll always be glad you did.

Scout

By J. Jones

Also by this author

The Chronicles Of Arkadia Series:

Destiny Of The Sword
Redemption Of The Sword
Fury Of The Sword
Last Stand Of Old Heroes

Anthologies:

Tales of Terror For A Dark Night

Scout

By J. Jones

"Four minutes, Sergeant," said the captain looking at his silver pocket watch for what must have been the hundredth time. He briefly glanced at the oval shaped photograph of his beloved wife inside the lid before snapping it shut again. Now was not the time for emotional weakness.

"Very good, sir," replied Sergeant Reed. He slowly started to walk along his section of the trench eying each man as he passed them, looking for faults. "Four minutes, lads."

The men looked nervous he thought, but then again they weren't really men; most of them were just young boys barely old enough to shave. Here and there stood an older veteran, though to earn that title all you had to do was survive a couple of battles and make it to your twenties.

The sergeant came to a halt halfway along his section and glanced towards the captain who was once again staring at his pocket watch. He too was barely out of his teenage years yet here he was commanding a section of forty men. The sergeant hoped that the young man was up to the task. Their lives were very much in his hands.

One of the young soldiers in front of the sergeant suddenly let out a cry of fright drawing everybody's attention including the sergeant's.

"What's the matter with you, Taylor are you afraid the bogeyman's coming to get you?" asked the sergeant stepping behind the soldier. Some of Private Taylor's mates laughed at their friend's embarrassment, lightening the mood and relaxing the nervous tension which had been steadily building ever since they were ordered to stand-to.

"No, Sergeant," replied Private Taylor his cheeks colouring, "I felt something brush against my leg and thought it was one of those giant rats."

The sergeant stared at Taylor for a moment and then glanced down at the ground where Scout, a black Labrador and their regimental mascot, sat attentively at Taylor's feet. Every so often he flicked his paw against Taylor's leg in an attempt to garner attention. It was something he frequently did. Taylor followed the sergeant's gaze his cheeks turning fully crimson when he realised that the source of his alarm had just been the dog.

"I don't know what you do to the Hun, Taylor, but you frighten me to death," said the sergeant shaking his head. "Besides, no self-respecting rat would want to come anywhere near you let alone touch you. Who knows what it might catch." The soldiers started to laugh again enjoying their friend's good natured discomfort. The sergeant reached down and stroked the dog's head and instantly started to smile as memories of his own sheep dogs back on his farm in Yorkshire came flooding back.

When he looked up again Sergeant Reed saw that the men nearby were all looking at him and smiling, obviously enjoying seeing a softer side of their normally hard-nosed NCO. That wasn't good for his image. "Eyes front!" he snapped, all business again. He patted the dog's side and straightened up. Then he looked over at his captain again just as the officer held two fingers aloft. The sergeant nodded.

"Two minutes, lads," said the sergeant. "Prepare to fix bayonets." All along the line the soldiers withdrew their bayonets and held them poised at the end of their rifles. "Fix…bayonets." The air was suddenly filled with clicking noises as the lethal blades were snapped into position. The sergeant glanced along the line and nodded with satisfaction.

"Sergeant," said Private Taylor half turning.

"Eyes front, Taylor. What do you want now?"

"What's Scout doing here, Sergeant? He should be out of the line by now."

"He's coming with us, lad."

Several of the soldiers who had been listening started to grumble and voice their disapproval. In a world of mud, death and deprivation, Scout was one of the few good things in the men's lives and the young terrier was loved by all, if only because he was a reminder of what was good in the world. The thought that he might be injured or killed did not sit well with them.

"You heard the captain earlier, lads; the Germans over there are all dead. Nobody could have survived that barrage. We're just going to stroll over there nice and sedately and Scout's coming with us. The old colonel wants the whole regiment moving forward. The Jocks to our right are going to be playing bagpipes as they advance and I've even heard that the lads to the left are going to kick a football to one another as they cross No Man's land, so don't you go worrying about Scout he'll be fine. There's no danger."

The sergeant swallowed nervously and hoped he sounded convincing. He hadn't lied to the men but he too harboured concerns as to whether all the Germans had really been killed. It had been a fierce and deafening barrage to endure that was for sure and it would be easy to believe that no living thing could have survived it, but still…

Private Taylor glanced down at the dog which had resumed pawing him once the sergeant had ceased showing him any attention and smiled. The young dog stared back at him, his brown eyes wide open and his long tongue hanging out of his mouth. Taylor was convinced the dog was grinning.

"Sergeant," said Taylor.

"What?" replied the sergeant unable to mask his irritation.

"If we're expecting the Germans to all be dead, why have we bothered fixing bayonets?"

The sergeant didn't meet the young soldier's gaze nor did he reply. He'd been wondering the same thing himself.

"Good luck, Sergeant," said the young captain as he sidled alongside Reed and held out his hand.

"And to you, sir, though if the artillery boys have done their work we've nothing to worry about have we?" replied the sergeant shaking his officer's hand.

"Quite so, Sergeant quite so," though the sergeant noticed how the captain couldn't quite bring himself to look him in the eye. "Thirty seconds," the captain added looking at his watch again.

"This is it, lads, thirty seconds," said the sergeant turning to face the men.

"Remember, no running, we're to make our way across No Man's land in an orderly fashion; the colonel will be watching," said the captain.

"But not joining us of course," said one of the soldiers with his back to the captain drawing chuckles from his mates.

The captain chose not to hear the comment and stared intently at his watch. A few seconds later he blew his whistle and the men immediately began to slowly climb out of the trench an action mimicked all along a two mile front.

Unlike previous attempts the first heads to appear above the parapet were not immediately met by a hail of machine gun fire and everyone managed to leave the trench without incident. Sergeant Reed looked left and right for malingerers and once he was sure nobody was shirking, he made to climb the ladder after them when he spotted Scout looking up where the men had gone and whimpering.

"It's all right, boy, I'll carry you. It's all very well saying that you've got to come with us but nobody gave any thought to how you'd get out of here did they?" Slinging his rifle over his shoulder, he bent down and scooped the dog up in his arms and was immediately rewarded with a multitude of kisses and licks to the face making the sergeant laugh.

"That's enough of that, boy. Come on we'd better get going or the captain will have us both shot for cowardice," and with that he started to climb the nearest ladder.

By the time that he reached the top the men were already fifty or so yards ahead of him. He put the dog down and after giving the sergeant one last look and an enthusiastic wag of his tail, Scout ran off after the soldiers, stopping here and there for a quick sniff.

The sergeant watched him go and then briskly started to follow.

"Well that's gratitude for you. He could have at least kept me company till we caught them up."

***

Fifty yards ahead of the sergeant, the men, led by Captain Frobisher, fanned out into a long line as they approached the German trenches. From where they stood it didn't look as if the enemy wire had been obliterated as they had been promised, but thankfully so far there had been no sign of the enemy.

"Looks like for once the brass weren't lying to us," Percy Kendall called over to his best friend Jimmy Taylor. They were now over halfway across No Man's land, the German trenches nearer to them than their own trenches. "Not so much as a single Fritz bullet has come our way."

"I know," replied Jimmy smiling. "Just as well because if they didn't know we were on our way they would by now. Listen to that racket." He inclined his head towards their right from where the sound of several bagpipes drifted across No Man's land.

"I like it," replied Percy.

"Really? You're not Scottish."

"No, nor is he but he seems to be enjoying it," said Percy smiling and pointed to Jimmy's feet where Scout was walking beside him cocking his head from side to side listening to the wailing of the bagpipes.

110

"Hello, boy, you made it then?" said Jimmy. The dog looked up at Jimmy and wagged its tail furiously. "You stick with me boy and you'll be all right. I'll look out for you."

The dog barked and then suddenly darted forward towards the German trench.

"Scout, come back boy wait for me," Jimmy called after him and quickened his pace, but the dog was already twenty or so yards ahead of him.

It was then that all of Hell erupted around them. The silence was suddenly shattered by the sound of numerous explosions accompanied by the rat-a-tat-tat of several machine guns. The Germans or at least some of them had survived the barrage it seemed and were now out for revenge.

Jimmy glanced right towards his best friend just as a shell exploded right on top of Percy, vaporising him in front of Jimmy's very eyes. Jimmy cried out as beyond where his friend had stood just moments before, scores of British soldiers were scythed down like wheat in a field.

Panic threatened to smother him. Should he continue forward or should he turn and run back towards his own trench? One thing was for certain, he couldn't remain where he was or indecision was going to kill him. He was still contemplating what to do when a shell exploded close by lifting him into the air before dumping him back on the ground with a thump, winding him. For a few brief moments he thought that he was going to be all right, that he had survived. Then all of the displaced dirt and detritus of the battlefield landed on top of him, slowly blocking out his light, choking him. He tried to move, to scramble free but the weight of whatever had landed on him was too much and his right leg and left shoulder hurt like Hell. His leg felt wet and just before unconsciousness claimed him, he realised that he was bleeding profusely. It was a miserable way to die.

He wasn't sure how long he'd been dead; it could have been minutes, hours or years. Time suddenly had no meaning. Why though if he was dead could he feel something around his legs? He could feel a scrabbling sensation and then a gentle pulling, though there was no pain. *Why would there be; you're dead?* he reminded himself. It suddenly dawned on him that what he could feel were the bloated rats that were one of the many horrors of the trenches, tearing at the flesh of his dead body. The thought repulsed him but at least there was no pain.

He had resigned himself to lying in that state until his entire body had been consumed when suddenly a chink of light appeared before him and then another and he suddenly found himself looking up at the bright azure sky. Something wet was lapping at his face until finally his nose, his mouth and then his whole face was uncovered and he felt a gentle breeze caress his skin. He began to choke, coughing up dirt and dust until eventually he was able to drink in several large gulps of fresh air. They felt good.

Not dead then!

More and more of his body was finding itself released from the burden of weight and he started to struggle and free himself from the burial mound upon him. Fresh waves of pain surged through his body when he tried to move his right leg.

Something began licking his face and he turned slightly and almost laughed with joy when he recognised Scout standing over him and fervently wagging his tail.

"You're alive, boy and so am I thanks to you," said Jimmy freeing an arm from the dirt and reaching up to pat the dog.

All around him he could still hear the battle raging and once or twice he even heard the sound of footsteps as men ran past him in a hurry. Whether they were friend or foe he had no idea. The explosion had turned him around and completely disoriented him.

He was by now free of his earthy prison but in a bad way. He knew he had to find shelter otherwise he could well find himself at the mercy of a German sniper if he started crawling around in No Man's land trying to find his way home. All he could do was find a crater and hide there and hope that a stretcher party, either British or German, eventually found him. He just hoped that it was soon as he could tell that he had already lost a great deal of blood.

He slowly began to crawl towards where he believed the British trenches were located but every inch he moved was pure agony. He was about to give up and take his chances lying where he was when he suddenly felt a gentle pulling on the back of his tunic collar. He twisted his head and was just about able to make out Scout's head as he grasped his tunic with his teeth and tried to pull the young soldier along. Jimmy instantly began to try and help, desperately ignoring the pain.

Some minutes later, Scout and Jimmy slid over the edge of a crater and tumbled down its bank, finally coming to rest at the bottom. Thankfully this was one of the few craters on the battlefield which wasn't filled with fetid water, toxic from the decaying bodies of dead men, horses and rats. So many men had lost their lives drowning in such places that command had passed down an order that British soldiers were forbidden to try and rescue any comrades who found themselves stuck in the mud at the bottom of such shell holes. It wasn't just the mud that was so lethal, but the dreaded Mustard gas would also linger at the base of these craters, choking and killing those who found themselves stuck in the cloying mud.

Jimmy lay on his back panting and staring up at the sky. The pain in his leg had subsided a little but he could still feel that it was oozing blood at an alarming rate. He needed immediate help or he would bleed out.

His battlefield bandages had been lost during the explosion and he looked round for something, anything which might help. Deciding that his best plan was to make some sort of tourniquet he was glancing round for something to use when something touched his left leg. Jimmy turned to look and smiled incredulously when he saw Scout standing there with a small stick in his mouth. It was just the right size for a tourniquet.

"Good boy, Scout." Jimmy gently pushed himself upright and took the stick from Scout's mouth. Then he tore a strip from his vest. The dog sat down next to him and watched, gently panting. Jimmy carefully tore his trousers to reveal the wound and it was all he could do to prevent himself from crying out in anguish when he saw the severity of the wound. Trying to remain focussed he gently wound the tourniquet around his leg and tied it off.

Almost fainting from the pain he then lay back against the side of the shell hole and closed his eyes. Everything was silent, the battle evidently over, at least for the time being. All he could do now was wait to be found. He just hoped that he would still be alive when help finally arrived.

With his left hand he reached out and gently started to stroke the dog who responded by briefly licking his face. Jimmy's last thoughts before he once again slipped into unconsciousness were that if it hadn't been for Scout he wouldn't be alive.

***

"Some men will do anything to get out of latrine duty won't they, Sergeant?"

"They certainly will, sir, especially the likes of Private Taylor."

Jimmy Taylor reluctantly opened his eyes and found himself staring up at the smiling face of Captain Phillips and the sterner visage of Sergeant Reed.

"Where am I?" asked Jimmy hoarsely.

"You're in Field Hospital 12, a few miles behind the front line, Taylor," replied the captain.

113

"You mean I'm alive?"

The captain laughed. "Just about, Private. You did the right thing taking shelter in that crater and fixing a tourniquet, otherwise things might have been quite different."

"How did I get here?"

"Some stretcher bearers found you whilst they were scouring No Man's land after the battle. They found you lying on your own at the bottom of a dry crater. Damn near missed you by all accounts as your uniform and body were so covered in dirt, but one of them saw your clean white face looking up at them."

"I wouldn't have made it at all if it hadn't been for Scout."

"What do you mean, Taylor?" asked the captain.

"When a shell exploded near me I found myself buried under a ton of dirt and couldn't move. I thought I was dead and would have been if Scout hadn't come back for me and dug me out. Then he helped drag me to the shell hole. He even brought me a stick to use as a tourniquet. Smartest dog I've known. Where is he by the way, I'd like to see him?"

"I think you've had enough excitement for one day, Taylor, you're clearly confused," said the captain. "It's good to see you've made it though."

"What do you mean confused? I'm not confused about anything. Where is he? I'd love to see him, sir. Please."

The captain and the sergeant exchanged a strange look.

"Scout's dead, Taylor. I'm very sorry," said the captain.

"How? He was right by my side. I was stroking him in the crater right up until I passed out. Surely the Germans didn't shoot him. Please God no!"

"He died from shell fire, son, just like a lot of your mates. Just like Percy Kendall," said the sergeant.

Jimmy stared disbelievingly at the two men. "When?"

"It was virtually the first shell to explode when the enemy attacked. It was quick, son, he wouldn't have felt a thing," said the sergeant.

"But that's impossible. I told you; he dug me out and dragged me into the crater. He was very much alive then," replied Jimmy.

"You were in a great deal of pain, Taylor and were probably hallucinating. Scout died leading our attack. Several men claimed to have witnessed his death. I'm very sorry. We all loved the little fellow but I know the two of you had a special bond. Try not to dwell on it now and rest up. You've earned yourself some Blighty time." The captain patted Taylor on his unwounded shoulder and strode off to visit some of the other wounded, but the sergeant lingered momentarily.

"But I saw him, Sergeant, I know I did. He dug me out. I can still feel the sensation of him licking my face. That's why my face was clean, why the stretcher bearers were able to see me. He must have known."

"I'm sorry, son, but you're mistaken." The sergeant nodded at the wounded soldier and then strode off after the captain.

Jimmy closed his eyes and began to weep.

***

A few miles further down the front line a British soldier felt a bullet tear into his shoulder and tumbled into a nearby shell hole. As he slid down the bank he desperately tried to arrest his slide but his momentum carried him down into the filthy and festering water stagnating at the bottom. He landed with a splash and although he immediately tried to pull himself free, the cloying mud was already sucking on his boots refusing to let him go. Bit by bit, inch by inch he began to slip deeper into the mud. The more he struggled, the quicker he sank.

All of a sudden he felt someone tugging at his collar and slowly he began to feel himself being pulled free. Someone was disobeying orders and was trying to save his life. When he was finally free he scrambled up the bank a little way before turning to thank his rescuer. However, to his surprise it was not a fellow soldier lying on the bank next to him but a large black dog. Not believing his eyes the soldier reached over and patted the dog's side before grasping its collar and peering at his name tag: Scout.

If he didn't know better the soldier would have sworn the dog was grinning.

Man's Best Friend

Sent By Nick Collins

Man's Best Friend

While our Maker was resting from His Labour
And He gazed on the world from above
He saw many poor lonely humans
With no one care for or love.
Now the Lord in His infinite mercy
Both tender caring and wise
Made a furry and four legged creature
With a tail and a pair of brown eyes.
A heart filled with love and devotion
From the moment its short life began
And God smiled down from heaven
On the dog He created for man.
Now you've listened to my story with patience
And you think sentimental old clod
But just you try spelling dog backward
It's the name of his maker. It's God.

Marmalade

By N. R. Phillips

Marmalade

By N. R. Phillips

You hardly see one nowadays but, once upon a time, when the fishing industry provided prosperity for Cornwall, the streets of St.Ives were full of cats. If you walked from Up'long to Down'long, by way of the Stennack, through Street-an-Garrow, say, and then along Fore Street and up to Carn Crowse, you might see fifty or a hundred of them. St. Ives was famous for its cats. They used to lie in the sun in doorways and up the flights of granite steps, or even in the middle of the road, for there wudn no traffic then, and hardly any dogs. Everybody had a cat. All my family, Uncles, Aunts, Great Aunts, Grandparents, had cats, and we always had cats in our house when I was a cheeld, although personally, being a birdwatcher and a gardener, I was never very fond of them. She, on the other hand, even though she's from up-country, loved them, and thought that no home was complete without a cat, so, like everybody else in St.Ives, we soon acquired one.

One? What am I tellin' of? One! We had four of the little...darlin's. But for now I'll tell'ee about just one. She was a beautiful Tortoiseshell called Marmalade who was what they d' call a schizophrenic psychopath, prone to spectacular fits. That cat was the most perverse animal that ever lived, and we grew to hate each other with mutual relish. Apart from always having her eye on the sparrows in the garden, she could smell a freshly turned and immaculately raked seedbed from a mile away. Yeah, quite!

She was one of they cats which rub themselves against people's legs in the hope that they'll bend down to stroke them and murmur a few words of endearment. Her immediate response to this affection was a loud purr, followed closely by a forward roll and an invitation to tickle her proffered tummy. As soon as people obliged, she ripped the flesh from their hands in an unprovoked attack. I tell'ee that cat was the most perverse animal that ever lived. She was like the beast of Bodmin – shrunk, and we grew to hate each other with mutual relish.

She used to sit on the fridge by the kitchen door and purr a greeting at visitors before taking a quick swipe with a vicious right hook as they passed. I felt obliged, as a keeper of a dangerous animal, to warn people of her savagery, but it wudn easy, for she was a beautiful creature.

'Oh! What a lovely cat.' The times I've heard that. As she rubbed against people's legs or sat on the garden wall, purring like a good one. I always told them, 'Leave her alone.'

'Don't touch her!' I'd cry, 'She's a vicious devil.'

Might's well talk to myself. Catty people are as obstinate as cats themselves. You can't tell them nawthen. You cean't train them.

'Oooh, She's lovely.' You've heard them. 'Come on den. Who'd a priddy puddy den?' Patting their knees or laps.

Cat lovers all seem to think they have the blood of St. Francis of Assisi running in their veins. 'Oh,' they say, 'They always know who loves them. They can tell. Can't you, puddy pus?' Pat, pat. You can alienate your cat-lovin' friends by telling them that their 'way with cats' as they say, is, on the contrary, merely the cat's way with them. If that Marmalade ever did manage to settle herself on somebody's lap, p'raps when I was out of the room, gone to the kitchen to make a dish of tay maybe, I knew there would be trouble, as sure as eggs is eggs.

Sooner or later the time would come. It would be 'Come on then pussy. Time for me to go. Down you get.'

Ha! Low growls, like the rumbling of Vesuvius before the great eruption, as she clung there with those threatening eyes half closed and claws slowly extending into the cloth of trouser or skirt, one set of claws after the other, gripping and relaxing.

'Then 'Come on puss,' as the growls became louder, 'you can't stay there all night.'

Don't you believe it, I'm thinking to myself. I would try to be polite, diplomatic even. 'I wouldn't pick her up,' I'd say, 'if I were you.'

I knew, from personal experience, that the only certain way of getting her off without personal injury was to rise without warning, preferably while she was still asleep, and eject her on to an opposite chair, or even through the window, with a lewd and suggestive thrust of the hips. This required skill and practice, not to mention a certain degree of ruthlessness not normally found in cat-lovers, yet readily acquired after a few months living with Marmalade. I have seen that cat hanging on to people's legs with ten claws while I strained to pull her off by the scruff of the neck. I have seen her clinging to people's stomachs as they struggled with putting their coats on, pretending she wasn't there, or that they didn't mind wearing a dangerous sporran in the streets. The worst time was when she took one of her celebrated one, two, left, right, slashes at a lady, who's lap was due for a rest, and one claw became hooked into her wedding ring. Before I got her off, the other nineteen claws had reduced the lady's hand to streaky pork. I tell 'ee, I wore leather gauntlets just to pour milk into a saucer for that cat.

Sometimes, if I knew guests were expected, I was able to remove her from the sitting room with bribery and deception, by rattling tins or a saucer in the kitchen and closing the door quickly behind her as she rushed in, not realising it was a trick. She soon became too crafty to fall for that one, however, and sneered at me in contempt unless there was the stench of 'Moggyvite' the most expensive and evil-smelling cat food on the market.

After losing several friends who flatly refused to enter my house unarmed, I thought of constructing a series of wire-netting tunnels – from the door to her saucer and in to the rug beside the fire – like they have between the ring and the lions' cages in circuses. I could have poked her with sticks or electric cattle-goads and been quite safe from attack. I wudn allowed to do it. My wife was the cat lover in our house, and she and the children threatened to partition off my end of the dining room and push my food though on pitchforks, so I abandoned the idea.

I must tell 'ee one thing about Marmalade in her favour. She was a good guard-cat. No burglar would get the loot through the door past Marmalade, for she enjoyed attacking people who were carrying things and couldn't see where they were walking. She would curl up on the doormat the very instant she thought someone was about to take something outside. At any other time the doorway was far too draughty for her liking. Under the pretext of self-defence, after people had accidentally stepped on her, she would attack their legs as a tiger attacks a tethered goat: teeth into an artery and a quick disembowelling job with the back legs. I have seen a man run a four minute mile with Marmalade swinging from his calf like a furry leech gorging itself on blood.

The only time I enjoyed the company of that cat was when she was having a fit. Her fits were one of the seven wonders of the animal kingdom, as spectacular as they were unpredictable. Had they been predictable I could have gone on tour with a circus and made a fortune from admission fees. She would begin with a few twitches, like one troubled by a flea, and suddenly take off: rushing around the room, leaping over chairs, across the coffee table and bookshelves, scattering all before her. I have never seen her make it along the ceiling, but many a time has she been literally up the wall.

Everybody scattered when Marmalade had a fit. The effect in a crowded room was devastating: people running and falling over furniture in a mass panic, women screaming as she ran up their legs in a blur of teeth and claws and squirts of widdle. She would achieve maximum havoc, with spilled drinks and flower vases, ripped curtains, fainting ladies, and then collapse in a twitching heap in the most inaccessible nook or cranny available, so that she had to be extricated with a shepherd's crook or a bit of bent wire.

Marmalade's most spectacular, and final, performance was unwitnessed in the dead of night, but the trail of havoc left behind was her ultimate insult to me, her lifelong enemy. Not only am I unable to describe the scene as she wrecked an entire kitchen, I am also unable to describe the climax of her triumphant exit but, in what must have been her most spectacular fit of all, she collapsed and died wedged against the hall-way door. She knew, I am quite certain, just how far the momentum of that last leap would carry her, and she probably died in mid-air, with her last squirt of widdle aimed at my carpet slippers. That cat also knew, I'm certain, that the back door was locked, with the key inside the door, and that the only way to gain entry to the kitchen was by mutilating her stiff corpse, jammed against the door, or by breaking a pane of glass.

I broke the glass.

Pussies Galore

By N.R. Phillips

Pussies Galore

By N. R. Phillips

You would think, after the trouble we had with that bleddy Marmalade, we'd had enough of cats. But oh no, not she, she had to have another one. Then another. And then another. Tha's three we had. All at once. Madness! We had a pure white one called 'White One', and two all-black ones, called 'Black One' and 'Fluffy One'. Well you can't call two of them Black One can 'ee. Black One is not fluffy. Although Fluffy is black. They are normal affectionate, perverse cats, but no fits, thank the Lord!

Although we have a garden, they also have the run of the house, except for the bedrooms. I'm very strict about it but I suspect She d' let them sleep on the bed when I'm not there. They like to be in the house at night, especially cold winter nights, unless they are already in, of course, when they'd rather be out. Best of all they like to be in, with the door wide open, looking out. They'll yell to go out and then stand in the doorway trying to decide whether to change their minds.

I know what you're going to say. But we tried a cat-flap, and the neighbour's Jack Russell used to drop dead rats on the doormat, so we have to keep it locked. After the trouble we had with Marmalade… that's what she was called, the one who had fits who came to rule the house, we are very firm, in a kindly way, with these three. We have developed a routine, what they d' call, to our mutual benefit and stick to it. They are intelligent animals, after all, and soon learn. Take the other night. I'd had a bath and a nice cup of cocoa and was lying in bed, just going off to sleep when I remembered the little darlin's.

'Are they blasted cats in?' I asked.

'Black One and Fluffy One are in', she said. 'No sign of White One. But he'll cry to come in when he's ready.'

'Yeah' I said, 'I'll bet he will!' And turned into the sheets.

Miss World was just about to slide in beside me when the fifth meeow from White One woke me up. I swore silently into the pillow, with a soft snore, feigning sleep.

'The little dear,' she said, calling my bluff. 'He's calling you.'

'He idn' callin' me,' I said. 'They are your cats, remember, not mine.'

'But you're their Daddy,' she said.

You can't argue against such logic, so I crawled out of bed, thinkin' the sooner I let White One in, the sooner I could get back to my dream.

'Don't put the light on, Dear,' she said. 'It hurts my eyes.' So in semi-darkness I struggled into my dressing gown, the one my maid gave me for Cresmas, but the cord was all tangled and through to one side. I couldn't be bothered to untie all they knots and let 'n all hang loose, like they d' say.

'Bring in the pussy box while you're down there, Darling,' she said.

'I thought you brought in the pussy box.'

'No, Darling. I put it out.'

'And why did you do that, Dearest?' I asked with my customary good nature.

'Because the cats were out.' she said.

'But you knew they would be coming in, Sweetheart.'

'Yes' she said, 'of course. But I put the pussy box out to be brought in. It needs some clean sawdust.'

'Git away!' I said. 'You could have mentioned it before we came to bed.'

'Hmm?' she said. A bit too dreamily, if you ask me.

'Never mind!' I said.

I staggered to the stairs and fell over the Fluffy One who was asleep on the landing. He yelled and ran into the bedroom and leaped onto the bed for the protection of his Mummy, swearing terrible obscenities.

The Black One was on the kitchen table, with her head in the milk jug. I shoo'ed her off and put the milk in the fridge. I opened the back door and called to White One. 'Come on puss.'

White One ran in… with half a mouse in his jaws. I rushed to the hall door to stop him runnin' upstairs and dumpin' the mouse on my pillow. Black One, seeing the door half open, ran out. White One cowered in the corner under a kitchen chair, growling defiantly over the mouse whose entrails, spread over the tiles, foretold seven years famine and plague in Mesopotamia. I grabbed White One, pulled the remains of the mouse from between his teeth

125

and threw them outside. Black One grabbed them and was about to run off into the night when White One rushed past me and leaped upon Black One to retrieve his prey.

Fur flew like soot and snow in a hurricane, you. I went out to separate them, felt the mouse entrails curlin' round my big toe. Flicked them off, and stubbed my toe on a garden gnome fishing for trout among the begonias. I picked up both spitting cats and limped back to the house. She came into the kitchen as I shoved Black One and White One through the door.

'The pretty dears,' she said.

Just as I was about to close the back door, Fluffy One appeared from the bedroom, slunk around the skirting board and slipped out behind my back. I rushed out after 'n, and, as I tried to grab him, tripped over the cord of my dressing gown and went sprawlin' into a bench supportin' a row of potted pelargoniums 'Caroline Schmidt' which were my pride and joy. I smashed every pot. As I tried to rise I pulled the watering can off the bench and irrigated my parts with a bit of good stuff, a mixture of water and horse manure.

'Whatever' she said in that sweet way she has, 'are you trying to do?'

'Go back to bed,' I said. 'There's a good girl.'

She went off in a huff, slamming the hall door, which frightened White One, who ran out.

I closed the door to keep Black One in, and took off my pyjamas which were smelling with the potential fertility of next year's crops. I put some milk in a saucer to keep Black One occupied. She wasn't very keen because it was semi-skimmed. I wrapped a kitchen towel around my waist in case the neighbours were about. They're from up country too and are bit, well, you knaw! I opened the back door a smidgin.

'Puss puss. Drinkies.'

Fluffy One walked regally in, tail in the air. I jabbed the door shut behind 'n.

This was where I started, I remembered, with they two black buggers in and that white devil still outside. The dressing gown and pyjamas were scenting the house, so I opened the washing machine and put them in. The White One jumped onto the outside windowsill and peered in, meowing silently, as if he hadn't seen me for a week, and didn't want to wake the neighbours. I slipped outside in the towel, did a hop skip and a jump over the cold paving stones and grabbed him. He purred loudly, and rasped his back claws down over my belly. Blood poured onto the towel but I ignored it and opened the door a fraction and threw White One in with a smooth underhand movement which would have done credit to Sir Francis Drake on Plymouth Hoe in 1588. Black One and Fluffy One were both drinking the milk, and White One joined them. They were all contentedly lapping, crouching like a pride of lions. I slipped furtively inside the door, slipped the catch on the lock and heaved a sigh of relief. Thank God for that, I thought. Now, I can go back to bed.

Of course, I would need another bath, a plaster on my toe, a drop of antiseptic ointment on my belly, possibly a new dressing gown and pyjamas, and a tetanus jab tomorrow but, with a bit of luck, I would be in bed by midnight and Miss World might still be waiting.

I went wearily to the stairs, making quite sure none of them followed me and that the hall door was firmly shut... and remembered the pussy box.

Went back to the kitchen like one in a dream. The three cats rushed through the door and went upstairs. I went outside, shut the back door to keep them in, and walked through the broken shards and potting compost from my beloved Caroline Schmidt to the shed, to get the pussy box.

It was pitch black in there. I groped about for fresh sawdust and found a handful of last night's pussy poohs in the pussy box. I ripped the towel from around my middle, hastily wiped my hands on it and threw it to the back of the shed in anger. Eventually I found the fresh sawdust, and walked naked in the night to the back door with the pussy box all nice and clean.

The door was locked, of course. For I'd slipped the catch when I thought they all were in. I stood there holding the pussy box while the three pussies looked at me from the inside windowsill.

I scraped some gravel from the drive and threw it up at the bedroom window, whispering loudly 'Let me in!'

My neighbour's window opened and they both looked down at me. I covered my parts with the pussy box, as if selling matches and ice cream in a cinema.

'Yow' I said, as casually as possible under the circumstances. 'Lovely evening. No sign of rain.' They withdrew their heads, and I saw the light go on in the hall where their telephone is.

In desperation now, I grabbed a large handful of gravel and threw it up at the bedroom window at risk of breaking the glass. The mouse entrails went up with them and slithered down the pane. I thought she would faint if she saw them, and I'd be out here all night but, eventually, she opened the door.

She saw my goose pimples, the blood oozing from my stomach and dripping from my toe but, not letting me through the door, 'Charming', she said.

She eyed my tray of sawdust, my smelly hands, and her nostrils dilated in an inquisitive spasm. She said 'Not today, thank you.'

'Very funny,' I said, and shoved past her into the kitchen.

Black One, Fluffy One, and White One, ran out.

You got a cat have 'ee.

The Secret

By Janice Bell

May every animal
Be aware of the
Angel by their
Side.

The Secret

By Janice Bell

Henri is a posh Spanish dog.

It is stamped on his dog collar POSH HENRI.

Henri is a lovely white terrier, one of the things that makes him stand out from the rest of the white terriers is his one black ear and his one black leg. Both on his right side.

Henri's family adore him, telling him all their secrets! It baffles them the way Henri looks at them, as if he could understand everything they were saying. Then they would stroke him lovingly. Well what they didn't know was Henri did understand everything they told him.

Something had been bothering Henri lately, he had heard his Mum telling some guests how she had picked Henri from a litter of puppies a gypsy was selling. Mum then said there were five, and it was awful as two had died.

"Well," continued Mum, "We had already picked our Henri."

The guest then asked Mum what happened to the other two.

"The gypsy told us they were going to a village in the mountains called Los Naranjos."

"What did they look like, the other two?" asked the guest.

"Identical to our Henri," Mum answered proudly.

So one sunny morning, after deciding to go and find his brother and sister Henri was waiting at the bus stop. The bus came along Henri read the destination on the front of the bus.

That's right he read the destination! The *Valley de Verdad*.

That will do, Henri thought to himself, I can walk the rest of the way to the village of Los Naranjos.

The middle doors opened ready to let the people off, that is when Henri jumped on. Quite a few people on the bus smiled and stroked Henri, so feeling relaxed Henri stretched out for the long journey to the Valley.

Henri blocked out the voices shouting around him, thinking only of finding his siblings, that got him wondering if they shared the same secret as him. Being able to read, and understand everything that was said to him.

Henri heard the bus driver calling out Valle de Verdad. Henri jumped off.

Spotting the sign to the village of Los Naranjos, Henri set off purposely.

The other dogs shouted out to Henri, some friendly, some hostile, he greets them all the same a smile and wave of his paw.

Way up the mountain surrounded by orange lemon and olive groves, Henri finds a fresh water stream, and decides to takes a break. Looking round he sees a sign, 1km to Los Naranjos. Great, Henri thinks not long now.

He doesn't have a plan as such, but Henri feels excited.

As he reaches the village of Los Naranjos, seeing a group of dogs he walks over. The dogs, not used to other dogs just joining them especially posh ones, all stare and lowly growl at Henri.

Henri cocks his head from side to side...

"Hi guys. No need for all that macho stuff, I am here looking for my brother and sister who look just like me."

The biggest dog of the pack steps forward and snarls

"Listen short bum .We don't do family! As for brothers and sisters dogs like us, don't even know our Mums and Dads. So on yer bike OK."

With that the big dog kicks Henri hard sending him flying.

Picking himself up, he turns around bravely glaring at the big dog.

Henri walked on thinking to himself, maybe this was not a very good idea.

Then he heard a loud, "Meeow" and a long hiss, looking around he spots a cat waving her paw at him hiding behind a garage door.

"Come in quick, quick!" she shouts.

Henri's eyes grow accustomed to the dark, it is then he realizes that the garage is filled with straggly feral cats, fear fills his little heart.

Miss Black Cat who called him in laughs while telling Henri.

"Don't be frightened. We are peaceful cats, I heard you ask those horrid dogs if they knew your brother or sister."

Henri nods his head *yes*.

"Well," Miss Black Cat continues.

"I don't know if he is your brother or not but there is a lovely local ownerless dog that is the spitting image of you."

Several of the straggle cats crowd around Henri making his fur involuntarily stand on end.

"Yes, Yes," the cats squeal. "Travi must be his brother."

"OK, follow me I will show you where he lives."

Henri nods his head enthusiastically pleased to be getting out of the garage.

Miss Black Cat checks out the lay of the land.

"All clear," she whispers. "Stay close to me."

Henri follows Miss Black Cat, across the main village road, the heat rising from the ground, past sun bleached little houses, leading down to a small dirt track path, the smell of wild garlic in the air.

Henri hears the fight before he sees the three dogs, the bone of contention being the big cow bone they were fighting over.

Miss Black Cat screeches, "H-E-L-L-O, H-E-L-L-O."

The three dogs look up, steam pouring from their noses, drop the big bone, glaring at Henri and Miss Black Cat.

Miss Black Cat bravely ignoring their angry looks announces, "This posh dog is looking for his brother."

The three dogs all stare aggressively at Henri.

Henri raises his paw.

"Hi my name is Henri," he said, looking at a dog who is the spitting image of himself.

The dog called Travi moves toward Henri, sitting down.

Travi rubs his eyes with his paws, then looks at Henri again.

He puts his paws over his eyes crying, "I don't believe it. Are you tricking me?"

Henri puts his paw around Travi's neck. "Nah, I am not tricking you."

Miss Black Cat screeches at the other two dogs who are looking bewildered. "Oi, dirt bags! Scarper, go on get lost. Leave them alone."

With that Miss Black Cat wriggles her fat bum running away squealing.

"Bye, Henri. Don't forget, ever need any pussy help, you know where me and my girls live."

Henri holding up his paw calls back, "Thank you, Miss Black Cat. Will do."

Henri and Travi walk down the little dirt path until they come to an orchard. Travi leads the way to a tree, telling Henri, "This is where I hangout and sleep."

Henri shakes his head in a mixture of sadness and admiration. Henri then shares with Travi everything he had heard his Mum tell his aunties, uncles and guests. Travi shakes his head from side to side, putting his paws over his eyes and crying. Henri puts his paw around Travi's neck holding him tight.

Travi, fed up with feeling sad jumps up shouting, "Well that's life, amigo, seems you, Henri got to be the lucky one eh."

Henri pacing up and down tells Travi, "I got a secret to tell you."

Travi looks right into Henri's eyes saying, "OK what?"

Henri staring at the ground says, "Well, um I can read and I understand exactly what humans are saying!"

Henri carries on staring at the ground, then he hears Travi whooping and jumping punching the air with his paws.

"You too!" shouts Travi. "I can read and I speak loads of languages. I don't believe it."

Both dogs carry on excitedly laughing and rolling around on top of each other.

After exhausting themselves Travi tells Henri, "Now I know we are hundred per cent brothers I must tell you, I think I know where our sister is."

Henri feeling emotional, eyes brimming with tears, asks Travi, "Are you sure?"

"Well," answers Travi, "She is the image of us with the same black ear and black leg on her right side."

Henri spins around and around thrilled at that news.

"Wait don't get too excited, Bruv. I will have to fill you in about our sister."

After Travi has finished telling Henri, he sits, gutted.

"Well," said Henri "I still think I would like to meet her."

"Your life!" answers Travi , shaking his head.

Travi starts walking while telling Henri, "No time like the present. Let's do it Bruv. Let's go and meet the mean queen of a feral girl gang, who may just be our sister!"

Henri, feeling out of his depth, proudly follows Travi, past the sun bleached little houses onto the main village road.

Henri, in his own little happy world, is totally oblivious to the big gang of ownerless dogs across the street.

Travi nudges Henri whispering, "Stay close to me."

Henri stiffens while crying out, "Oh not those horrible dogs again. That big dog kicked me really hard up the bum."

Both dogs then start laughing.

"Oi, Oi here come the laughing princesses," shouts the big feral dog.

The rest of the gang crack up laughing then the big dog runs across the road at high speed, closely followed by his laughing gang.

Henri moves swiftly behind his brother. Travi, puffing himself up stands his ground. The feral dogs are sniffing and snorting lowly growling spoiling for a fight. Poor Henri realizes not for the first time that day he is terrified, so copying his brother, he puffs himself up hoping to look tough. Sadly it did not work his poor little legs buckled PLOP down he goes.

The feral gang move in surrounding Henri, pushing, nibbling his tail, barking loudly.

The big dog shouts at Travi, "So this is your posh princess brother." He points to Henri curled up on the ground.

"Yeah that's right!" shouts back Travi. "And guess what, we have a sister."

The big dog takes a while to compute this information.

"Yeah that's right!" Travi shouts

"We have a sister and you know who that is."

The big dog and his gang move back.

Poor Henri removes his paws from his eyes realizing maybe he is not going to die just yet.

Travi, really bravely shouts at the gang, "Well, dirtbags not so tough now are you?"

One of the feral dogs asks, "Who's their sister?"

"I will answer that one," said Travi. "She is queen of the feral girl gang!"

The dogs their eyes open wide, all gasp and run away. Sitting on a wall nearby Miss Black Cat and her girls all screech and clap their paws.

"You OK, mate?" Travi asks.

Henri now getting the hang of street life answered, "Yeah! Cool, Bruv."

Henri follows Travi through fields and along little mountain roads until they come to a rickety old gate with a sign saying, LAVENDER FARM PRIVATE PROPERTY.

Henri gives Travi a look that said, 'What now?'

Travi puts his paw over his mouth while slowly pushing the gate open making a huge creaking noise. Henri feels scared. Travi keeps on walking, so

Henri keeps on following. After a while Henri bravely whispers to Travi, "Is this where she lives?"

"Yes. This is Queenie's territory." Travi nods

That's when they heard the creaking getting louder and louder. Henri feels his little legs collapsing again, the creaking is so loud now Henri holds his breath. That is when he sees his sister running towards him wearing a dog collar made of lavender with a pack of wild dogs following her. Seeing Henri and Travi the Queen of the gang stops. Holding up her paw, the others stop. She stares long and hard at the brothers, then going up close to them she barks then kicking dirt over them shouts, "What you want, Bruv?"

Travi looking straight into her eyes tells her,

"We are your brothers!"

Silence. The queen carries on kicking dirt at Henri and Travi then the others join in.

"We should leave," calls out Travi and Henri agrees.

"OK, Bro. What now?" asks Travi as they sit under a tree near the lavender farm.

"Well I think we should go back later, let her calm down a bit. Did you see the way she looked at us? She knows for sure."

"Hope so," replied Travi

"For a sister she is not very welcoming."

Both dogs laughed, curled up and had a much deserved siesta.

Waking up feeling refreshed the two brothers quietly and bravely go back to the Lavender Farm. It didn't take long before they came across their sister curled up on a cushion on an ornate little chair. Travi indicated to Henri that he would try to attract her attention. Travi moved closer to the chair. Then not being able to stop himself he loudly farts. Travi and Henri look at each other then their sister and burst out laughing.

The feral dog Queen removes herself from her little chair trying to suppress her giggling.

"So, guys, you think we are related?"

Travi nods his head saying, "I think you had better listen to posh Henri he will tell you the whole story."

Queenie nods her head from side to side, Henri and Travi both laugh.

"That is definitely our sister!"

Henri tells Queenie most of the sad story. When he has finished, Queenie, laying on the ground, paws over her eyes doesn't move.

Henri continues, "Queenie, there is one more thing and this will be all the evidence and proof you will need, that you are our sister."

Queenie looks up at Henri her eyes brimming with tears.

"Can you read?" Henri asks.

Queenie jumps up.

"OMG I don't friggen believe it! Yeah I can read, Bruv."

All three go for a group hug, kissing and laughing with joy.

"So what's next?" asks Queenie.

Henri answers shyly, "Would you like to come and live in my house with me and Travi?"

"What like a real family?"

"Yeah," answers Henri.

"But what about your owners? Won't they mind us crashing with you?"

"No, my mum is always reading those self help books to better herself, my Dad is already a better person so nah, they won't mind, in fact they will love it."

Queenie takes off her lavender collar leaving it on her little ornate chair, "Okidoky lets go."

Outside the Lavender Farm, sitting on a wall as still as a statue, is Miss Black Cat. Seeing the three happy dogs, she calls out, "Good luck little family."

The three dogs thank Miss Black Cat. Posh Henri is so happy he is fit to burst.

Running down the hill they pass all the old village ladies sitting outside their pretty sun bleached houses, who smile and nod their wise ole heads at the three white dogs, all with one black ear and one black leg and a massive secret.

"Right," Henri calls out, "Let's catch the bus home!"

It's a Dog's Life

By Fran Scott

I hope readers will not just see the sadness of this story about my very special four legged friend, but also see the very great joy she gave to all who met her. It was Rosie who gave me the inspiration to write about her life, and Rosie who helped me on my life journey.

It's a Dog's Life

By Fran Scott

I can't really remember much about my birth mother, and my father was never around. But I did inherit a lot of Spanish Water dog from one of them, so I was quite curly, black and white in colour, and of course I loved water. I first met my special human family quite suddenly one sunny day in March. My mother's family had left me on some steps in a place I did not recognise, but although I really missed my mother, I was soon distracted by a rather handsome blond haired boy who apparently lived around this place. I followed him and his human family everywhere, and I sat on the steps of the place where he lived when it was night time, and his human family gave me food. One day, not long afterwards, I followed him and his human to another house nearby which had trees and a garden, and my boyfriend and I raced and raced around the garden laughing and playing together. There was a lady there who asked about me, and who did I belong to, and my boyfriend's human said I was hers if I wanted her. So the lady picked me up, and she cuddled me tight because I was a bit scared, and we sat on the steps where I let her know silently that my name was Rosie. So from then on, she became my human Mum.

What good times we had, me and my Mum. We walked around lots of hills, and I could run and play and find lots of things to smell. There were lots of places with water, so I could get wet and have a great time playing. My new human Dad was really good at playing with me with ropes and balls. I could hang on to the rope with my teeth, and he would lift me up in the air. He invented a new game – " I'll get that doggie" which involved a lot of running and chasing, and usually ended with me running underneath a trailer

138

that was parked in the garden, where I managed to dig quite an impressive hole. Of course I had to growl when I did this. Sometimes we went on holidays and stayed in a big green tent, and I played on a sandy beach and swam in the sea. Usually I mostly liked to catch sticks that my Dad threw into the sea, and although he once got me right into the water to swim, I really preferred the stick catching game, and we often went to the beach just so I could play stick catching in the sea. It was my favourite game.

Now I wouldn't really want you to think I was always a good girl. I often rolled in lovely smelly things I found, and my Mum had to give me a bath, which although I loved water, somehow I was never that keen on that. I really loved people, but I did take exception to one or two, and I was not so keen on all the dogs that went past our house. There was a path above our patio, and a lovely ramp to race up and bark at people I didn't like the look of, or say hello to the special people I loved. One day a small white dog came by with its family, and I have to say I took an instant dislike to this dog, so I gave it my full on loudest bark, and raced up the ramp to see it off. Well, it was a bit of a wimp, and promptly fell off the path on to my Dad's shed, slid down into a rose bush, and then on to the ground, by which time I was back down to give it a seeing to. My Mum was very cross with me, and I was banished to my bed. I think the white dog was ok, but it was certainly a lesson for it not to cross my path again!

I did of course run up my ramp to say hello to my special people, my part time mum and dad, and my boyfriend's mum who always tickled my tummy the best of anyone. One year my mum and dad's family came to stay with us, and afterwards, even though they had not been back to see us for a really long time, I heard their voices before anyone saw them, and I ran up the path to meet them, and my mum was really surprised.

Now I did have some lovely beds to sleep in, but one day my Mum came home with a really special soft and cuddly pink bed. I took one look and instantly fell in love with it, and made my Mum laugh because I got straight in and smiled at her. Not very long after this, my blond haired boyfriend called for me. He was staying with another man and lady, who were also my part time mum and dad when my mum went away. So I loved them and I loved my boyfriend, and my mum and part time mum took us for a lovely long walk. On the way home my boyfriend whispered to me about a special place he knew to go exploring, and when our mums were not looking, we raced off. They were busy talking, so didn't notice we had disappeared, and when we heard them calling us, we were too busy having a good time to run back to them. I think we must have disappeared for a long time, but it seemed to go very quickly for us. Our mums had walked home and were getting our Dads to come and help look for us, but when we realised how long we had been, we thought we had better race back. Now my Mum was not pleased to see me at all, she was really cross, and to make matters worse, when we got home she took away my new pink bed, and I had to have one of the old ones. Of course the next day she forgave me, and I had my pink bed back. I never ran away again!

Then one day we all went on a long journey in my family's car. I had my own bed in the back, and it was my own special place where I could sleep or look out of the window. We stopped in lots of new places where none of us had been before, and everywhere we went I was very well behaved as my Mum had taught me how to be a good girl, and how to behave in public places. One of the places we stayed in was a beautiful hotel, and we all slept in the same room which had an outside balcony where I could watch the sea and all the people going by. I loved it all. My mum got talking to a lot of different people who asked her about me, and I think she was quite proud that I was always a good girl. We went to a big castle by the sea, and while my Dad went into the building, I sat outside with my Mum. Lots of people came to say hello to me, and one of them was a tiny little girl who was smaller than me. She was with her Dad, and so to make it easy for her to stroke me, I rolled on to my back with my legs in the air. This made her squeal with laughter and my Mum can still remember this today.

Then we went across the sea on a big boat with lots of other cars. I had to stay in my bed in the car, and when we got to the end of the sea, we were in another place where, when my Mum and I went out walking, I discovered some new animals – rabbits! They were just perfect playmates for me as they liked to run and so did I. Usually they ran faster than me because I don't think mum was too happy about me catching one. There was another place we went where there were so many rabbits I didn't know which way to look. Unfortunately these rabbits lived in the same place as some other animals called sheep. So sadly I had to be kept on my lead after I had caused mayhem with these sheep who were panicking about me chasing rabbits. One day we all went to a place by the sea, and the weather was cold and it was raining, so eventually my mum and dad found a lovely place where they could eat cakes and drink some of the stuff they liked. We sat near to a lady I really liked, and she made a fuss of me. I am not bragging, but I was quite pretty and people seemed to be drawn to me. When the lady left, she told my mum that she suffered with an illness that made her ears ring, and that the time she had spent with me gave her a lot of peace. We were away for a long time visiting different people, and then we went back across the sea. We stayed in a house which really scared me, and even though the people there had a dog as well, I just could not take to them, and I never left my Mum's side. I just knew there was something wrong here, and my Mum stuck up for me when the lady said I must be timid. Little did she know how timid I was NOT!

Eventually though, we finally returned home to the places I loved most, and to my favourite water places. Occasionally we went walking with some other people, and one of the places we visited was my most favourite place of all. There were lots of trees and amazing smells, and I always had to race off with my nose almost permanently on the ground. Added to that, there was a big lake which was a beautiful turquoise colour where after all the running I could catch sticks my Dad threw into the water. Every time we went there, I just couldn't wait to get out of the car.

I must mention that sometimes my mum and dad went away for what seemed a very long time, or sometimes just for a whole day, and I was a lucky girl because I stayed with my part time mum and dad. My part time dad knew about the "I'll catch that doggie"game, and he also took me for walks, and the lady gave me food and cuddles. They were really special to me, and their house was my second home. But when my mum came home I was always so excited I ran around and barked and made a big fuss, and never gave a backward glance to my part time family.

Now when I was nearly six years old, I did a silly thing. My Mum, Dad and I usually sat on our terrace at night when it was cool, so that we could all look at the stars. As you know I loved chasing things, and one night, even though my mum had said NO, I just had to run after something that I heard near our house. You must understand that when I heard noises like that a red mist came down, and I just had to see what was going on. My mum did not see me go, and she did not see me fall. She had no idea that I had really hurt myself badly, and she rubbed my leg and cuddled me and put me in my beautiful pink bed. She didn't understand that I was hurting because I didn't cry, but she did say we would go to the vet when it was open the next day. But then my back legs stopped running or walking, and my mum and dad took me in the night to the animal doctor in our town. I stopped with him and he made me feel much more comfortable, and the next day my Mum and Dad came to visit me. The animal doctor said I could go home with my family that night, and my Mum stayed up with me holding my paw, and we slept one last night together. In the morning we sat on the steps and my mum cuddled me just like she did when we first met. She took me to another special animal doctor in the big city the next day, but he knew that he could not make me walk or run again. My Mum and Dad knew I would not be happy if I could not walk or run, so we all had to say goodbye. I looked at my Mum and my eyes glistened like stars with all the love I had for her, and she held me tightly when I went on my big journey. When my mum and dad got home without me, they knew I was still with them in our house, as they could keep smelling me, and when they went to pick up my ashes I let them know I was there again. They took my ashes, and went with my part time mum and dad to the special lake where the water is turquoise in colour. They found a special place to leave my earthly remains. They all said goodbye and they all cried.

So I had to leave my friends and family, and now I live in another place where it is always sunny, and I can run and play with a new family, and other dogs and cats who all know my mum. There is even a white rabbit here who used to live with her, so I don't chase him, and we all talk about the great time we spent with her. I know my mum really misses me, and to cheer her up, one day I left one of my curls on her mat where I knew she would find it. She keeps it in a special place. I still visit my mum, and I know that sometimes she sees me out of the corner of her eye. We both know that one day she will come and find me in this other special place, along with all the others who have lived with her. You see, a dog's life never ends.

My mum and dad had some really special years with me when I lived on the earth. They think it is really sad that other people don't understand about a dog's life, or a cat's life, or any other animal's life. I don't know what sentient means, but apparently people are only just realising that all of us creatures have feelings, and that we live forever in another place, after living on the earth. Please tell everyone that we can make you all so very happy. Please love us properly and then we can then love you back a hundred times more. We can make your life very special when you spend time with us. You can make our lives really special when you look after us and treat us in a good way.

It was a great dog's life for me.

From La Marina to La Finca: Paddy Comes Home

By Sandra Piddock

Also by the author

Sandra Piddock is a freelance writer and blogger who divides her time between Algorfa on the Costa Blanca and Bigbury Bay in Devon. She specialises in writing about all things Spanish, and runs her own website, sandrainspain.com.

From La Marina to La Finca: Paddy Comes Home

By Sandra Piddock

It took me a long time to persuade my husband Tony that we should have another Dog in Residence. 17 years in fact, from the day our beloved Border Collie Patch bid his farewell to this life at the grand old age of 17. So, why did he finally change his mind? I really don't know. On New Year's Eve, 2013, when four of our friends pitched in and pleaded my case, he got stroppy and said something along the lines of 'Never mention dogs to me again, or else,' yet less than three months later, we were collecting Paddy from the K9 Club Animal Charity in La Marina, Spain.

Maybe it was down to the lucky red knickers I was wearing on New Year's Eve, or perhaps it was because he was having one of his 'What's Sandra going to do when I die?' moments. He's been having those quite regularly since he hit 70 – he's 81 now, so there have been a lot of them. Anyway, we were sitting in the sun on Sunday 16 March, 2014, and he suddenly asked me if I still had the *Coastrider*.

That's the local English language newspaper for the Torrevieja area, and I wondered what he wanted it for. Tony said he wanted to look in the Classifieds, and I got a bit concerned then. You see, in Spain, along with the adverts for plumbers and removal men, you're likely to see adverts for – er – ladies belonging to the oldest profession in the world. I wondered whether Tony was perhaps trying to hasten his demise and wanted go out with a smile on his face, but what he said was even more of a shock than if he'd asked me to book an appointment with 'Janine, busty, long-legged blonde, 37. Will meet at your place or mine.' His next words were:

'Pick yourself a puppy from one of the animal shelters.'

First of all, I ignored him, thinking I'd heard him wrong. When he repeated it, I went indoors to check the levels on the whisky bottle. That didn't seem to have 'evaporated' since last night, so I went back to the sun loungers, and asked him if I'd heard him right. Apparently I had, because once again, Tony repeated the words I'd resigned myself to never, ever hearing.

I checked the *Coastrider*, and the *Courier*, and the *Round Town News*. And there were puppies aplenty – too many puppies, because I wanted all of them, yet none of them actually said to me 'Take me home – I'm yours.' Well, they couldn't have, could they? Not from the newspaper and not in person, but you get the idea, I'm sure.

I was quite happy to wait for next week's papers, but once Tony wants to do something, he wants to do it now, or even yesterday. He can be so impatient. A religious friend of ours once suggested he should pray for patience, and he said, 'Please God, grant me patience, and I'd like it immediately.' And he was only half joking! But I digress.

Anyway, Tony suggested we look on the websites for the various charities, because he reasoned there were so many dogs needing homes, they probably couldn't put them all in the newspapers. Before I did that, I tried to do my duty as a Responsible Wife and told Tony that if we had a puppy, it would be hard work for a couple of years. Wouldn't it be easier on us to get an older dog?

Tony's answer to that was that with an older dog, we might not know what sort of life he'd had before, or how it could affect his temperament. He had a good point, actually. Although we don't have any young children at home, we do have grandchildren and great grandchildren in England, and we didn't want to put any of them in danger from an unpredictable dog. As Tony said, if we started with a puppy, even if he'd had bad experiences, we should be able to get him over them with love and attention, and train him so we had the kind of dog we could take anywhere.

We wanted a dog that wasn't too big, but what we didn't want was what we call 'a rat on a string.' Yorkshire Terriers and Chihuahuas are okay if they belong to somebody else, and we'll make a fuss of them, like we do with any dog, but it would never be our choice for a pet. Having had a Border Collie, we did think some sort of Collie cross would be ideal for us, and when we went to the K9 Club website, we saw Paddy – or Teddy as he was called then.

It was love at first sight for both of us – now I'd found a puppy who looked at me and said "Take me home – I'm yours.' I think the main reason we fell in love so completely was that he reminded us of Patch. He wasn't pure Border Collie, but there was more of that than anything else, and he had a white blaze on his face, white socks and a white chest. When we actually hunted out our old pictures of Patch, he wasn't much like him at all, but at the time, it struck a chord.

Now we'd found our boy, I was impatient to get to him before anyone else did, so I called the kennels, even though it was Sunday teatime. I reckoned that looking after dogs wasn't a 9 to 5 weekday thing, and I was right. Kayla answered the phone, and told me all about Teddy, as she'd called him. And what she told me made me cry, and made me want to bring Teddy home and make it up to him for the rotten start he'd had in his short life.

A week earlier, Kayla had been exercising some of the 11 dogs they had in the kennels at the time near the canal. The dogs got excited, and Kayla thought she heard a noise, so she investigated. She found Teddy, covered in mud, freezing cold and whimpering, by the side of the canal. Next to him was what she presumed was his brother, and he was already dead. The puppies were no older than 6 or 7 weeks, and Kayla said if she hadn't found Teddy when she did, he too would have been dead by morning.

Kayla had no way of knowing whether the dogs had been thrown in the canal and managed to struggle out, or whether they'd just been left on the canal bank. She was distraught that the puppies had not been left at the K9 kennels, which backed onto the canal, because then both of them may have been saved. She took Teddy home, bathed him, fed him and, because he was so tiny and cold, she allowed him to sleep with her in her bed, rather than putting him in the kennels with the other dogs.

By now, I was determined to have Teddy – although he would need a name change. As Tony said, he had no intention of standing at the top of the steps and shouting 'Teddy, time for dinner!' I mean, you never know who might be passing, and if somebody sees an 80 year old calling his Teddy in for dinner, they might decide to call the Ambulancia to take said 80 year old to a place of safety.

Kayla called him Teddy because he was such an affectionate little chap, even though he'd had such a rotten start in life. As we were chatting about names that evening, we thought a Spanish name such as Pedro, Paco or Pablo would probably suit him, but we decided to leave the naming ceremony until we'd actually met him.

The next day, we headed for the K9 Kennels bright and early. When we arrived, Kayla took us to met Teddy. He was in a pen with two other Collie cross puppies who were a few weeks older than him, and twice his size. They were bounding over him as if they were on elastic, knocking him over, and he was just getting back up and back in the fray. I fell in love all over again, and although the other puppies had on their best 'Pick Me!' faces, I knew that Teddy was coming home with us, and so did Tony. When Kayla let him out of the pen, he just strolled over to me, wagged his tail – which was as long as him with a little white tip – and gazed at me. I picked him up, and he nestled in my arms. Teddy was home.

Kayla explained that we did not have to make a donation unless we wanted to, but we wouldn't have felt comfortable about taking Teddy without giving something to them to cover his keep for the week he'd been waiting for us. And we were so pleased to have found him, so we handed over €50. I don't think many people give as much as that, because Kayla was over the moon. She filled out a receipt for the donation, and as I signed it, I noticed the date – 17 March, St Patrick's Day. There was that number 17 again. And we finally had a new name for Teddy. On such a day, what else could we call him but Paddy?

That's When The Big Fight Started

By Ann Patras

This was written when I was learning to write my book. If you liked the poem you might like my book, which is now available on Amazon. It is called *Into Africa: with 3 Kids, 13 Crates and a Husband.*

That's When The Big Fight Started

By Ann Patras

Here is a story to be told, it happened to our Mummy.
She's still quite cross about it all, but we thought it was funny.
Our Daddy had an accident, he nearly burnt the fryer
He put the pan outside to cool, but should have put it higher.
Next morning our dog King got up and thought it was his birthday
From head-in-pan his fur stuck up, like Mummy's real bad-hair-day.
You see, he'd licked the pan all out and cos it was so greasy
His head and shoulders got oiled up – it wouldn't come off easy.
Mum thought she'd better bath the dog but he was dead against it.
He leapt right out, jumped on her bed, and absolutely drenched it.
And then he ran into the yard and jumped amongst the flowers
Whilst Mummy stayed inside to clean – she said it took her hours.
My brother said "Let's go and play." So off we went to Peter's
His Mum was buying ice-cream cones and said that she would treat us.
I didn't know my brother Tim had left our gate wide open
The dog came out to track us down, well that's what he was hopin'.
'Twas only some time later when we noticed King was missing
Our neighbour said he'd seen him trotting past, when he was fishing.
With everyone out calling him, on bikes, in cars and trucks
We found him on the pig-farm road, all covered up in muck.
But by the time we all got home the day had turned to night.
When we walked in our Mum just screamed "My goodness, what a sight."

What happened next was quite a scene, now Daddy's broken hearted.
He said that Mum must bath the dog. That's when the big fight started.

The Cat That Fell From The Sky

By Rosemary Lewis

Writing has always interested me and two years ago I joined a creative writing group. Putting my story forward for inclusion in this book has served two purposes – it has given me confidence in my writing and as I love all animals I have the satisfaction that some of those that need support will benefit too. Thank you.

The Cat That Fell From The Sky

By Rosemary Lewis

It is often said that fact is stranger than fiction. This is a short documentary of events as they happened (with just a little artistic licence).

Opening the front door I let myself into the house.

"Hello, I'm home."

It was twelve thirty on a beautiful sunny day. I am pretty sure that would be about the right time as my job as a Receptionist finished at twelve fifteen and my journey home took approximately ten minutes. Is this an important fact, something that has a bearing on the story you may well be asking and I have to admit that it isn't. It's just my usual way of waffling and padding out a story so that you the reader won't feel too 'short changed'.

The back door was open, and my husband called to me,

"We're outside."

We, being him and our dog Bonnie. She was a large, elderly yellow Labrador who was so laid back she was almost horizontal, only coming to life when in the presence of food or if she got the chance to throw herself into water. She loved swimming.

Stepping out onto the patio I was surprised Bonnie didn't come to greet me as she usually did; instead she was standing facing the corner, her nose almost touching the wall, her tail tucked between her legs. This lazy indifference to my homecoming, even for her, was exceptional.

"What's the matter with Bonnie?" I asked, looking at my husband who was viewing the scene with a wry smile on his face. My eyes follow his gaze. There sitting on one of the garden chairs was a beautiful looking cat; its' blueish grey coat shining almost silver in the warm sunshine. Now, I had grown up having cats around me; my mother was constantly rescuing them and as a family we were well known in the neighbourhood for taking in waifs and strays of the feline world. Over the years I had shared my home, and bed with many, but never one as beautiful as this one.

"Oh what a lovely cat. Whose is it?" I walked over, putting out my hand and in anticipation it lay down, purring gently as I ran my hands over its' silky fur. Bonnie eyed the two of us warily then slowly slunk off into the safety of the house. My husband laughed.

"She doesn't know what to do with herself. It keeps rubbing itself around her legs so she's been standing in the corner for nearly ten minutes trying to pretend that it isn't there."

"Oh poor Bonnie, I don't think she's ever had contact with a cat before." I went into the house and made a fuss of her before going back outside and repeating the question I'd asked earlier.

"Well - whose it?"

"I've no idea. I was kneeling down here mending a puncture on the bike, I turned round to pick up a spanner and there she was, just sitting there watching me. I've no idea where she came from, one minute she wasn't there and the next minute she was. It was as if she'd just fallen from the sky."

"Ha, ha, very funny!"

At this point I should perhaps mention (and, yes this bit *is* important) that our house is one of four small cottages set in the (relatively) middle of nowhere - our nearest neighbours being half a kilometre away.

Knowing none of them owned a cat of any description, I still made a point of contacting them all and asking the question. No one could help. Then I noticed something. The cat had ten stitches or so in the tummy area and as I could see that she was a female I assumed that she had recently been spayed.

"I have an idea. This shouldn't take long to sort out" I said confidently.

I had already consulted my cat book and it was obvious from the pictures in there that this cat wasn't just any 'ordinary' cat, but a pedigree Burmese Blue. This meant that she would have been an expensive purchase. Someone had looked after her well and had also spent money on having her spayed. She hadn't been dumped or abused, I was sure of that and her owner must be frantic with worry. Time to put my idea into practice.

Two hours later and I had contacted all the vet's within a fifteen mile radius. I repeated the same story over and over but no one had recently done

152

an operation on such a cat. They all said that as she was a Burmese Blue they would remember if she had been one of their patients at any time. She definitely hadn't. I was flummoxed.

It was time for Bonnie's afternoon walk. Setting off down the track in the direction of the woods we hadn't gone more than a few yards when the cat caught up with us. I tried to shoo it away but it insisted on joining us, amazingly trotting alongside us all the way down the path, through the little copse and into the meadow, past the stream and back home through the fields. A good two miles.

While I had been out walking; my husband had driven to the supermarket and purchased some cat food. We fed both cat and dog at opposite ends of the kitchen and kept guard in case there were problems. There weren't any and after eating her food and drinking some milk the cat made herself comfortable on the settee and went to sleep.

Early that evening I took her to my local vet's to see if he could offer any advice. He confirmed that she was indeed a Burmese Blue and also that she had been spayed - probably about ten days earlier as her stitches were ready for removing. He estimated her to be about ten months old. I paid for him to give her a check-up and to remove her stitches, and I recall him commenting that he had never come across gut of that type before. I was not the standard black gut that is usually used in sutures but it was coloured in some way. I don't think the vet believed my story that we had only just found her because she acted as though I had been her owner from day one, lying in my arms without a murmur whilst he snipped out her stiches.

No Facebook or Twitter then, and much as I hate social media I have to agree that if there had been such things, then she and her owner would have quickly been re-united. There was no microchipping either so I really had no direct way of finding out who she belonged to. Time to involve the Cats Protection Society. The local office had no report of any missing cat with that description but they kindly offered to contact other branches in the surrounding areas for me just in case.

"Where is the cat at the moment?" one lady asked me.

"Oh she's sort of draped herself around my shoulders" I replied.

I had a feeling, that she, like the vet, didn't really believe that we had only known this cat for a matter of hours.

"We'll make more enquiries in the morning and circulate an advert on your behalf, and then we'll be in touch."

Two weeks passed. The Cat's Protection never got back to me. We put an advert ourselves in the local papers, made some posters, putting them up in the local post offices and along the canal bank just in case she had 'jumped ship' so to speak and come off a passing canal boat. Everything we did drew a blank.

The cat, who by this time I had secretly named Sophie (due to the fact that she appeared sophisticated) seemed happy and settled. She was still joining us on our walks with Bonnie or sometimes meeting up with us on the way home. It was uncanny how she knew what direction we were coming from as we often varied our route. I would dearly have loved to have kept her but Bonnie was utterly, utterly miserable, and also I had to take into account that adjacent to our garden was a train line. Normally it was a 'goods train line' with approximately three trains a day but at weekends this would increase to more than a dozen on both Saturdays and Sundays, and these, were not slow moving 'goods trains' but fast intercity trains. So not the best sort of home environment for an inquisitive feline. What could I do? Sophie was a lovely cat and I now felt responsible for her. I had to find her a good home.

Racking my brains, I suddenly remembered having a conversation with a lady called Pat a couple of months previously. She, like myself was a member of the village drama group and she had been telling me that she had lost her cat some months previously.

The cat called Sandy had simply gone out one day and never returned.

"I don't want any more, it's too upsetting *and* I'm quite appreciating a 'hair-free' house."

She had been adamant, but I was desperate. It was worth a try.

I rang her number.

"Hello 786241, John speaking."

This took me a bit by surprise as John her husband, worked overseas on contract work in Saudi Arabia, and I didn't know that he was home on leave. We had a general chat about this and that and then I explained why I was calling. I told him the whole story, finishing by asking would they like to adopt Sophie if no one came forward to claim her. I was pleasantly surprised that he didn't instantly dismiss the idea.

"Mmmm, might a good idea. It would be company for Pat while I'm away. We did talk about getting another cat but decided against it as she was so upset about losing Sandy. We'll have a little chat and I'll get back to you."

Five minutes later the phone rang.

"Hello, it's John again. Can we come and meet Sophie?"

And that is exactly what they did. I had no need to plead or cajole - Sophie charmed them just like she had done us. One look into those beautiful aquamarine eyes and both of them were hooked. I explained why I had called her Sophie and said that they of course could choose a different name for her if they wanted to.

"No, it suits her. It has a quite a regal tone to it. Sophie! Sophie Hamilton. (Pat and John's surname was Hamilton.) Come on Miss Hamilton. Let's get you home."

John, with two tins of cat food and the cushion she'd been sleeping on, led the way out to the car. Pat followed carrying Sophie wrapped in a towel.

Three days later I had a call from a tearful Pat.

"She's gone! I went outside to peg the washing out and Sophie squeezed out of the door before I could stop her."

"When was this?"

"Oh, just after breakfast, about three hours ago. I don't know what to do."

"Give me half an hour and I'll come over and help you look for her."

I was just about to leave the house when the phone rang.

"Hello its Pat. She's home. A woman who lives several doors away came to ask if I could get my cat as it was asleep on her bed. She doesn't like cats and seeing Sophie lying there just freaked her out."

***

Over the years I would occasionally call in to see her and would find her reclining on the settee on her own special cushion, or she would be asleep in the airing cupboard. It was quite apparent that she had found her forever home.

Sophie turned out to be quite a hunter. Sometimes when she had been especially naughty, I would receive a call from Pat informing me in an accusatory and disgusted tone of voice.

"*Your* cat has had a mouse in the kitchen and left a terrible mess."

She used up several of her nine lives.

Visits to a neighbour's garden where she located the fish pond gave her many happy hours watching the fish as they darted tantalisingly in and out of the rocks. And of course one day the inevitable happened, unable to stand and watch any longer she made a sideways swipe with her paw, overbalanced and fell in. All this was observed by the neighbour who upon retrieving her then took great delight in returning the sodden Sophie to Pat.

"That'll teach her a lesson she won't forget," he had said, grinning.

"It didn't!"

It wasn't her only contact with water. As Pat's house backed onto the canal, Sophie could often be found lying on top of the brick wall that separated the lawn from the water. Pat, who was in the garden one day, saw her roll off the wall and land with a loud 'plop' into the canal's murky depths. She was quickly 'rescued', towel-dried and in less than an hour she was defiantly sitting back on top of the same wall.

Once, languishing in the sunshine on top of a neighbour's car, the owner, unaware of his feline hitch-hiker drove off with her balancing on the roof. Further down the road Sophie was observed jumping daintily off when he slowed down going around a corner. Another time she wasn't so lucky and was found lying unconscious at the side of the road. An emergency dash with her to the vet's seemed necessary but after a thorough examination she was given the all clear and sent home to 'take it easy'.

She had a fascination with vehicles and once ended up at a garage four miles away. A tradesman had been doing work at one of the neighbouring houses and Sophie being Sophie had climbed on board his van and was spotted on the forecourt of the garage when he had stopped to get petrol. Pat had bought her a collar with her name address and telephone number on so a quick phone call from the garage soon had them re-united and no harm was done. Everyone admired her and she took all the affection in her stride.

Sophie's personality was a real mixture. She was serene, regal, lazy, aloof, stubborn, loyal, affectionate, loving, inquisitive, feisty and so, so sophisticated.

She was, as John had hoped, good company for his wife whilst he was away and despite Pat's grumblings about Sophie's (disgusting) hunting excursions, she loved her dearly.

Towards the end of her life Sophie sadly became blind. The vet said that she might or might not adapt to the condition but one night it would appear that she had tried to jump up onto a chair in the kitchen and had fallen and broken her leg. A decision had to be made and it seemed that the kindest thing to do would be to have her put to sleep.

Seventeen years had passed in the blink of an eye.

She was a very special cat and lived a long and happy life with people

156

who adored her. Where she came from I will never know but whenever I think of her it is always as Sophie - 'The cat that fell from the sky.'

THE END

It would be wonderful if anyone could shed light on the mystery as to where Sophie came from. Perhaps someone reading this, lost such a cat all those years ago. She was found in Fradley, Lichfield, Staff's. U.K. (1986/1987? – not sure of the year)

The Strays Who Came In From The Cold

By Margaret Burrows

The Strays Who Came In From The Cold

By Margaret Burrows

It's April 2015 and spring is evident throughout the Valle de Lecrin, Andalucia, also known as the Valley of Happiness. There's only one problem though, this year, right now I'm not at all happy!

Two years ago we arrived at approximately the same time and were determined to do something about the endless litters of kittens we were faced with every time we came back to our traditional Spanish house which is situated in a small pueblo in the valley. Cats run wild, find food where they can, some from locals and others from regular tourists. They obviously serve their purpose well for we rarely see mice let alone rats. However when the population gets out of control, and it often does, the cats either get poisoned, their kittens dumped in the river or put in plastic bags and dumped into the bins by the local residents. There is little chance of rescue as the bins are emptied every single day without fail. I'm an avid animal lover and this, for me, was very upsetting, hence I decided enough was enough, I would catch as many as I could and personally pay to have them spayed. This of course meant befriending feral cats, pretty dangerous I can tell you. I've lost count of the number of livid scratches that covered my hands and arms not to mention the deep bite I received in the palm of my hand resulting in a quick visit to A & E. Caging them was another matter altogether. I have had a cat literally climb a bathroom wall where I had had her cornered and poo all along a wooden beam. I felt so sorry for her she was so frightened and couldn't know that I was not going to harm her. Most of the time I could just entice them in a cat box with food as they were hungry all the time. Over the last 2 years I have personally paid for 12 cats to be spayed and I feel good about that. At that time I wasn't aware of what we now know as "Spay Days". Mass spaying by sympathetic vets at half the price. Anyway I digress...

Where we live we have a little luxury by means of a splash pool which is accessible through a door just across a narrow path from our front door, literally 6ft away. For privacy the pool area is surrounded by extremely high walls of differing levels. There are 3 steps leading up to the oval shaped pool and the floor surrounding the pool is made of concrete and decorated with typical Spanish tiles. A real suntrap where in the evenings you could just to sit, read and be seduced by the aroma of our jasmine bush.

One evening 18 months ago after taking a stroll around the village I heard the loud continuous meowing of a cat, and because every sound in the village is amplified, was unsure from where it emanated. After a short recce I decided to open our pool gate and in the darkness saw a black cat pacing up and down. It took me a while to realise to my horror that she was calling to a kitten which had somehow fallen into the pool and was desperately swimming for its life. I immediately caught the bedraggled little kitten, went into the house and wrapped the poor trembling mite in a towel. It wasn't more than 3 or 4 weeks old. After half an hour or so it had calmed down but started crying for its Mother. I went back into the pool area, where she was still pacing and calling for her kitten so it seemed the most natural thing to put her kitten down in front of her. Oddly the Mother just whacked it with her front paw and refused to have anything to do with it. I waited patiently for a good hour for them to bond but it wasn't to be, the Mother cat completely ignored the crying pleas of her kitten. I left the kitten in the pool area that night quite safe on the patio level in a tiny box lined with 2 soft towels. During the course of the evening I regularly checked up on both of them. The kitten was heartbreakingly crying and calling and although the Mother cat seemed to recognise the call, did nothing. I had no choice but go to bed and just hope and pray they would be together in the morning. Sleep did not come easily that night.

The situation was no better in the morning, in fact the mother cat had totally disappeared and I was left with a lonely, crying and by now very hungry tiny black kitten. I wasted no time and bought a syringe from the chemist and some condensed milk from the local supermarket ready to be watered down. Needless to say I actually relished the thought of hand rearing a totally black kitten and promptly named it Zulu.

Over the next couple of weeks Zulu kept me busy with regular feeds and as he was still soul-renshingly crying I kept him outside during the day to see if Mother cat would return to claim her kitten. Sadly she didn't and after a week Zulu stopped his crying and finally accepted me as his new Mum. As the weeks went by Zulu was turning into a most adorable, mischievous, lovable, lap kitten. I was utterly and totally smitten.

Early one morning, a couple of weeks later, as I was looking out of our first floor balcony window over into the pool area, I was shocked at what I saw. The black adult cat was on top of our 20ft wall at the back of the splash pool accompanied by 3 equally black kittens. II watched fascinated and noticed that she was calling to them to follow her down to the next wall level to the right of the pool which meant a drop of approximately 6ft. Far too high for a tiny kitten. They crept to the edge looked down at their Mother and thought the better of it. No way were they attempting that drop. For safety reasons she had obviously had all her kittens in the derelict house at the back of our pool and somehow Zulu had possibly slipped off the wall and luckily fallen into the pool and not onto the hard tiles.

The next day, to my astonishment one of the kittens had actually managed the drop totally unharmed and was running around the wide ledge of the lower outer wall of our pool area. I watched as Mum then took it in her mouth and put it behind our large shaded bougainvillea. We watched fascinated at her attempt to encourage the other two down, but they would have none of it. After a couple of days we realised that Mum was spending less and less time with her "elevated" kittens and concentrating on the grounded one, regularly grooming and feeding it. This was a bit of a worry as the remaining two kittens were by now quite hungry and vocalising that fact. So we hatched a plan. I would climb a ladder, stand on the lower wall and put some food out for the two kittens to entice them to come to the edge of the higher wall. As they were feral and not surprisingly wary of humans I would have to quickly put my hand around the kitten and scoop it into the air and push it safely into the pool where my husband could retrieve it. To my surprise it worked like a dream and Mum and kittens were soon reunited. Zulu by his time was thriving and had just started eating solid food therefore noticeably larger than his siblings. Again I tried to reunite the family but poor Zulu was just ignored or whacked by his Mum so I finally gave up and from that day forward he became for all intent and purposes our cat. To this day I will never understand why she abandoned Zulu.

Because we have to leave Spain every year for a couple of months during the winter mainly to see our respective families and my ageing mother, it was not fair for Zulu to become a house pet. I feed many other village feral cats and over the years they have become accustomed to this routine. Fortunately in my absence they are fed by ex-pats in the village or friendly locals. They seem to know instinctively when I am back, waiting for me to feed them outside the back door within a couple of hours of my return. A previous litter produced two lovely cats who I named Barney a big ginger Tom, and Blue a large all black Tom. They are very good natured animals and when Zulu was old enough I introduced him to them. Fortunately they took to Zulu straight away, so I had no qualms about keeping him outside with them during the day. After all he would have to learn to fend for himself during the winter and what better way than in the company of two strapping males. Needless to say they had all been castrated. Zulu grew into a wonderful sleek, slim tall elegant cat who liked nothing better than to sit on our lap and creep into our bed at night. Seriously that cat was so stealth we never felt him and he never woke us up. He was an absolute joy.

Now with so many black cats around, you'd think it was difficult to differentiate between them all, especially in the dark. Zulu we knew, he was tall and slim and had a very high pitched meow. His two sisters were easier to define. One had a white tip to her tail and the other had a few white hairs on her chest and a large white patch on her underbelly. Blue was also quite easy, he was a large sturdy adult Tom who was prone to head-butt you, playfully of course. The mother of Zulu we had spayed down on the coast as soon as her kittens had been weaned and the vet cut the tip off her ear as an identification. This apparently is common practise.

Because of my affection towards Zulu I was naturally apprehensive to leave him, but I really had no choice and could only hope that he had learnt enough from his pals to survive the winter, which that year, thankfully wasn't too cold. Prior to us leaving we noticed a coloured female with a collar, handing around. She was lovely, really tame so I thought nothing of it as she was obviously someone's pet.

After a couple of months away and getting regular positive feedback from our colleagues in the village we finally arrived back eagerly waiting for our furry family to reappear. True to form, within half a day they were all back wanting their regular feed, except Zulu. Would my worst fear be realised? Two days passed and no Zulu. One morning, whilst lying in bed, I heard this high pitched meow. It was unmistakeably Zulu's meow. I ran downstairs, opened the door and she immediately pushed her way through all the other cats who were patiently waiting for their morning feed and headed for the utility room where she had always been fed. But she had changed. She was still the slim, sleek tall Zulu we raised but she wondered more. She would sometimes disappear for 2/3 days at a time, heavens only knows where, but would eventually come back to stay and sleep with us for 3 to 4 days before leaving us again. We soon got used to her routine and slowly I stopped fretting that we may not see her again.

The lovely coloured female with the collar who we thought was someone's pet had also turned up. This time minus her collar and worst of all, heavily pregnant. For a couple of days she tried desperately to come into the house but I kept taking her back outside on the occasions when she succeeded. Like I said, she was heavily pregnant and early one evening, I don't know how it happened but I found her laying on our sofa nestled in amongst our cushions. With a heavy heart I put her outside again. We were about to go out to our local bar/restaurant when we heard one almighty scream. As we were quite used to the cats having an concessional disagreement, we thought nothing of it, until it happened again and this time it seemed to come from outside our front door. I looked down from the balcony and to my horror and dismay saw that the female was giving birth on a neighbour's old cushion outside our pool door in the alley. The poor thing. I immediately went about putting her and her then only kitten into our pool area where it was safe from any predators. I found a cardboard box which I kitted out with newspaper and old towels. I also covered the outside with dustbin liners to make it reasonably waterproof as the forecast was not good over the coming days. At least she would be comfortable and could give birth in private. Had she been feral she would have found the most inaccessible place to have her kittens and nobody would have seen them until they were about to be weaned, at approximately 4-6 weeks old. This is what I find abhorrent with the Spanish attitude in getting rid of kittens in the most inhumane manner as I previously mentioned. They are the cutest fur-balls ever at that age, even ferals.

So off we went on our night out content with the knowledge that she would be totally undisturbed and we could enjoy ourselves without giving her another thought, well, almost. There was no way that I could go to bed that night without having a look in to see how she was doing, and to my surprise she had given birth to four more tiny, beautiful, helpless kittens.

As there were a considerable amount of ferals already in the village and in our area alone the territory was already occupied by a family of around 8 cats and with the neighbouring territory you could count on another 6, so therefore an addition of five would have been too many. Had she been feral only two would possibly have survived. Not only with regard to feeding and spaying but also hygiene would have been an issue as they poo'ed and pee'ed quite indiscriminately. We therefore decided to semi tame the kittens, that's to say get them used to humans yet be wary at the same time, and to try and find them homes. We had 200 posters printed with their pictures including their names and ages. Yes, we named them. The two ginger kittens were Biscuit and Marmalade, the two black and white kittens were Oreo and Oscar and the all black one was Dusty. We even named the mother Fiver, since she had five kitten. Not very imaginative I know, but it suited her. We travelled to three towns and asked local businesses if they would display the poster, we asked vets, bars and restaurants. I must say they were all sympathetic and very helpful. We also posted the pictures on as many Animal Rescue sites on Facebook as we could find, and waited and waited and waited. All in all we received only 2 enquiries. One was from a Spanish woman who just gave up trying to make herself understood as my Spanish is not at the level where I could translate the local dialect being spoken at 100 miles and hour.....and the other was from an English couple living in Spain, but we had already gone back to the U.K.

During all this time Zulu and Mazimo came and went as they pleased being no trouble at all and giving us huge pleasure.

In soon dawned on us that re-homing these wonderful five kittens, who were now semi tame was going to be a no brainer, so, after being spayed we decided to completely let them loose in the village and hope that their adopted family would be able to teach them to hunt and be afraid of the humans they didn't know. Their mother, at that time was herself still only young and also had trouble fending for herself as a some stage she must have been domesticated. I continued to feed them daily until 1 month before we were due to fly to the U.K. During this time I reduced their feed to once a day only and during the last week I cut out a feed on occasional days. When I look back, I am surprised at how I found the strength to do that as they continued to hang around crying for food, and playing. But I knew they had to learn to be totally independent from me.

So with a heavy heart, they day in early November finally arrived when we had to go back home. I left a ton of biscuits for the cats and plenty of water. For days on end I thought of them. I emailed my friend who said she would keep an eye on them and she regularly reported back. As time went on I got more involved with my life back in the UK and busily prepared to visit my daughter in Australia for 3 months. We actually stayed away longer than usual this time as within 3 weeks of returning to the UK I attended my son's wedding. It was mid April before we longingly returned to our lovely village in Spain eager to meet our feline family again. Unbeknown to us the local council were working on improving the alleys and stairs in the upper part of the village where we live and it took a good 3 to 4 days before the cats slowly returned. The noise and disruption would have scattered the whole family. We have now been back for 3 weeks and we are missing four of our dear friends. Zulu is one of them and I am totally gutted. The other three were part of Fiver's litter. Oreo, Oscar and Marmalade. I walk around the village and surrounding countryside regularly still hoping they are safe and will come and visit me again.

Although I am very sad, the remaining family are brilliant company, funny, playful and I rest in the knowledge that they are happy. Somehow I just know that some stray, be it cat or kitten will find its way to me again and I'll never, never turn them away.

The Tortoise And The Hare

By Valerie Collins

Valerie Collins is a writer who has lived Barcelona for a very long time. She shares the magic of Catalunya, Spain, creative writing and the English language via her books, articles, stories and workshops. She is co-author of the popular book that distils the essence of Spain: In The Garlic: Your Informative, Fun Guide to Spain. Currently she is putting the finishing touches to a novel set in a vibrant magical Mediterranean city.
Her website is www.valeriecollinswriter.com

The Tortoise And The Hare

By Valerie Collins

Tortoise had become so demoralised by other, faster, nimbler animals bullying him that he lost all his self-confidence. Instead of feeling calm and unhurried and savouring every instant of Now, he yearned to be fast like cool, streetwise Hare.

It's not good to be a tortoise, he told himself.

So Tortoise went into a decline, sitting around moping and beating himself up.

One day Frog hopped by. He shared that Tortoise should find help: there were many personal growth gurus hanging out in the forest and he would surely find one who could gift him with a tool or process that would turbocharge his energy and take his life to the next level.

But Tortoise was too depressed to reach out to Frog or to anyone.

The next day Owl came to visit and perched on a branch close by. He told Tortoise that affirmations were the thing.

"You don't need to move from the spot," Owl said. "It's a no-brainer. Give it a whirl: you have nothing to lose."

So Tortoise spent all day affirming: "I am cool. I am fast. I am streetwise," until he was screaming with boredom.

Then Fox came by and told him that affirmations were a waste of time: the real deal was visualisation. So every day Tortoise visualised his legs getting longer, his shell shrinking, his ears growing. He visualised himself leaping along the forest trails, feeling lighter than air.

But nothing happened.

Hedgehog told him the way to go was to have his chakras balanced:

167

Squirrel did that kind of work, Hedgehog said. So Tortoise went to see Squirrel. But Squirrel said that Tortoise's energy was so slow and dense and his chakras obviously so sluggish that she couldn't even locate them, let alone rebalance them.

Tortoise was now desperate, so Squirrel referred him to Elk who did something called Quantum Healing.

Elk said the key was to enter the quantum portal, where Hare was an unmanifest part of the infinite field. There, Tortoise could dissolve his tortoise energy into the field, and then align and resonate with Hare energy, which would then collapse its wave function and manifest on the material plane.

This only confused Tortoise even more. Now he was totally desolate and totally screwed up.

Finally, Old Fairy came pottering along, leaning heavily on her cane, and asked Tortoise what was wrong.

"Can't you just wave your wand and turn me into a Hare?" Tortoise said.

Old Fairy tutted and shook her head. "This is a learning and growth experience. No magic bullets," she said. "Tell me: what is your worst hurt?"

"Being slow: being a tortoise."

"Being a tortoise is worthless, right?"

"Yes, it is. For sure."

"Tortoiseness is worthless."

"Exactly. Life as a tortoise just isn't worth living."

"Can you accept that?"

"No. I hate it. I can't bear it."

"Look around for evidence that being a tortoise is valueless."

"I can see it all over the place. I can't run. I can't even walk properly. It's crap being a tortoise."

"Splendid. That's it."

"What do you mean that's it?"

"Can you accept that?" said Old Fairy. "Can you really feel it? All your pain comes from your efforts not to feel that pain."

Tortoise writhed in emotional agony, clawing at himself, banging his head on the forest floor. Being a Tortoise was unbearable. Un.Bear.A.Ble. The pain was so bad, he would die.

And then suddenly he couldn't writhe and bang his head anymore. In fact it was really rather boring. What a waste of energy. With a sigh, Tortoise let go and crumpled into a heap.

And then it hit him. It was true. His unhappiness didn't come from being a tortoise. It came from fighting being a tortoise.

And so Tortoise settled into a blissful calm, revelling in every moment of Now, chuckling compassionately at the ever more frenzied, stressed and jetlagged superluminal Hare, who often managed to arrive before he'd even set off.

And that is how Tortoise became the coolest, wisest, and most respected animal in all the forest.

Dog's Angel

By Sarah Luddington

Also by the Author

The Prophecy
Vampire
Seelie

The Knights Of Camelot Series (10 Volumes)

Sons Of Camelot (3 Volumes)

Unforbidden: The Queer Collection

Dog's Angel

By Sarah Luddington

"I'm sorry, Mr Simons, I know it must be difficult but I have to take a statement before we can pursue this and it's important we do it sooner, not later," said Sergeant Dale Smith.

"I know, I know," I murmured. "It's just hard to concentrate, the damned pain..."

"Let's start again. You've been a victim of bullying."

"I've been a victim of hate crimes," I said, frowning and my face cracking open again. He winced as blood began to trickle down my cheekbone.

I tried to calm down. This wasn't the policeman's fault. In fact he'd been lovely, scraping me off the street, stopping the worst of the bleeding and driving me to the hospital rather than waiting for an ambulance. He'd stayed with me as they'd begun to stitch me up and give me heavy shots of antibiotics.

I drew in a deep breath and began to talk in a more rational manner. "I live in a block of flats on the Moonhill Estate. My neighbour two doors down doesn't approve of my lifestyle. I've made complaints but he's never actually hit me, just threatened to do it. I have them logged. It became so bad my ex-boyfriend almost begged me to move in with him and his new squeeze. I'm lucky to have good friends."

"Why didn't you move?" Sergeant Smith asked.

"Why should I? It was my home first," I said. "Just because I'm gay doesn't make me a pervert, paedophile, or –"

"It's alright, Richard, I know what people can say," Sergeant Smith said, cutting me off and stopping the tears before they began. His hand rested on the bloody bandages wrapped around my hand and arm.

"I just don't understand it. I'm not hurting anyone. I've never hurt anyone," I said, the emotion akin to something I felt at thirteen, the first time I was beaten up for being 'queer'.

"Try to stick to the facts, we can deal with the fall out later," he said.

"You're being very nice to me," I whispered, sniffing heavily. He searched for a tissue and handed me several.

"It's my job."

"Not in my experience," I said.

"Well, we aren't all the same," he said.

I looked at him. Tall, dark blonde cropped hair, green hazel eyes and a strong jaw. He was handsome. I managed a small smile. "No, we aren't all the same." I couldn't help the small sparkle of flirtation from whispering outward to brush again him.

He grinned and shook his head. "The attack, Mr Simons."

"Yes, Officer," I said, obedient now. "I was walking home, under the flats; he was coming the other way with a dog. I didn't know he had a dog. It was a Staffordshire bull terrier. I love dogs. He had one of those collars on that actively dig into the animal's neck when they pull. The dog was too thin and something in its eyes made me want to turn around and run. I've never felt so much hate and hurt coming off another creature." I shuddered. The dog scared me far more than the man on the end of the lead.

"The bloke began shouting insults and yanking on the dog's chain. The poor animal started barking like a lunatic. The next thing I knew the bloke just released the animal and it's flying for my face. I managed to get my arm in its mouth. I rolled over to get the beast under me and I held my arm deep inside its mouth. That's when you came around the corner and hit it with your Tazer, by which time the bloke had run off."

"I didn't see him, it was too dark. I just heard the dog, the abuse and your screams," Sergeant Smith said.

"What's going to happen to the dog?" I asked.

Smith sighed. "He'll be put down."

"That's not fair. It isn't his fault. He was just reacting to a terrible situation."

"It's the law. He's a dangerous dog. He's attacked someone and drawn blood."

"He doesn't know I'm gay. He didn't do it because he hates me," I said, indignant for the dog's sake.

Sergeant Smith managed to raise a smile. "I know he doesn't care if you're gay, but he can't be trusted with people, not now."

"It's not fair. He shouldn't have to suffer for someone else's cruelty. Can I vouch for him? Can I have him?" I asked. For some reason the fate of this poor, unloved, hound made my heart ache in pity.

The Sergeant's eyes widened. "You aren't serious. Listen, Richard, these dogs, they're made, bred, tortured into fighting machines. He's not a household pet." I could see and even understand his concern but something kept murmuring inside me about that poor animal who had, after all, been forced to hurt me.

"No, he's a neglected, abused, misused and misunderstood animal who needs some kindness. I know how he feels," I muttered.

"It'll take a few weeks for the paperwork to be processed. I'll see what the authorities who deal with the dogs say. I also think you need to consider the implications of owning a dog who's already tried to kill you."

I grunted and we continued to wait for the NHS to grind me through the system.

***

"You sure about this?" asked Dale for the hundredth time in the last few days.

"Completely sure," I said. The stitches in my face had been removed that morning. I'd been given every healing cream in existence by my friends who were variously, "Horrified, darling" or "It's a tragedy beyond compare" or my favourite from my ex-boyfriend – "God, Richard, who's going to want you now?"

The scarring was spectacular; half my right cheek had been torn from my face, only Dale's intervention keeping it intact. Fortunately the policeman didn't seem to mind the damage and had become a regular visitor over the last few weeks. I still couldn't quite work out if he was interested in me or felt sorry I'd been victimised and had a girlfriend somewhere I didn't know about. I didn't want to scare him off so I'd acted against type and been patient. I liked him, really liked him.

We were in Dale's car heading for the registered dog's home the police used to keep animals secure. He drove calmly and with confidence, the same way he did everything. I took the opportunity to enjoy the view and it wasn't the one outside the car.

When we arrived at the pound I felt the nerves begin. To be honest I

173

didn't really understand why I was doing this – I had a horrible suspicion it might be because everyone said I shouldn't, couldn't, wouldn't and therefore I was doing it regardless.

I was right about one thing. It wasn't the damned dog's fault.

"Here to see the Staffy in the Simons case," Dale said to the woman behind the counter, flashing his warrant card at her.

"You the fool who thinks he can rehabilitate the demon dog?" she asked, flirting with Dale. I could hear it in her voice, even though I had my back to her while browsing through the items for sale.

"No, I am," I said, smiling to give her the full effect of the scars.

She went pale, her eyes widening and I thought she'd puke all over the paperwork. "Sorry, right," she said, nodding too much.

One phone call and a short wait later we were being escorted into the training yard by a different girl.

"We use this space to help the dogs learn different skills, such as walking on the lead, meeting other people, other dogs, even cats if we have one confident enough in the cattery. We can teach them games to play and generally make sure their stay here is at least bearable. We can also bring one person to one dog without upsetting the entire pound. Makes life a bit quieter for the neighbours," she said and she smiled.

"You seem to enjoy your job," I said.

"I love it," she said. "Your boy is a bit of mystery though."

We walked into a central courtyard, not too large and brick built to a height of about ten feet. Dogs don't scale walls on the whole but they clearly weren't taking chances as a wire fence ran around the top.

"More secure than Auschwitz," Dale murmured.

I didn't reply, my nerves not helped by the aggressive environment.

"We can go you know. There are hundreds of other dogs that need a loving home you don't owe this one anything," Dale said.

"I owe him a life because someone stole his, the way they keep trying to steal mine," I said. "We're both victims of the real animal in this case."

"Alright," Dale said.

The gate clicked open and the girl walked in with the Staffy on the other end of a thick lead. He was tall for his breed and very, very stocky. A dark brindle colour with small ears set back on his head and small eyes. He also wore a thick plastic muzzle. He came closer to us, to me, and the scars on his nose and head were clear to see.

174

"Here he is," she said, almost apologetically. The dog took one look at me and Dale, dragged the girl across the small yard and sat with his head pressed into the corner and his back to us.

"Does he have a name?" I asked.

"The others don't like him because of what he did, but I feel sorry for him so I called him Mouse."

"Mouse?" Dale was incredulous. He chuckled.

"Mouse it is," I said.

"He's not going to move. He's broken in the head," Dale decided.

I ignored him and walked toward the Staffy. I opted to sit down with my back to the wall and within arm's reach. I saw Dale's broad shoulders stiffen. I was too close for his sense of comfort. To be honest I was too close for mine.

"Strikes me you have one choice, Mouse, you come home with me or I leave you here to face the needle alone. Want to try living with me rather than eating me?" I asked the dog. His head was sunk into his shoulders, his ears were back and he trembled slightly, there were scars covering his haunches. "Mouse? Home?"

The dog swung his large heavy head toward me and whined. He really was an ugly looking brute.

"Home then?" I asked him. The black nose quivered as he took in my scent. "You remember me?"

Mouse wagged his long thin tail just once.

"Come on then," I said, standing up without touching him.

Mouse moved with me, his head still low and his ears still back.

"Looks like I have a dog," I said.

"You going to brave the lead?" Dale asked. He eyed Mouse the way policemen eye drunken young women, trying to work out which bit they can grab without being sued for harassment.

I bent and picked up the end of the lead. Mouse turned his head to look toward my face but not actually at me. He didn't growl. I took this as a good sign. The four of us left the yard and returned to the shop to fill out paperwork.

Mouse lay at my feet and didn't move until I said, "Time for home."

He rose and padded at my side to the car. I had the lead but it didn't do much leading. Dale opened the back of his car, which I'd furnished with a dog cage. Mouse sat and looked at it and his head sank further into his shoulders.

"Doesn't like the back of the car," Dale said.

"He doesn't have much choice," I said. "I don't want you arresting me for infringing some law or another."

Dale tried not to smile. "I don't know, handcuffs might be fun."

I shot him the least amused look I could manage while thinking about handcuffs and the lovely Dale.

"Mouse, this is the only way you get to travel. We aren't walking across the city," I told the dog. "Look, I have toys." I reached into the car and brought out a squeaky chicken.

It squeaked when I squeezed its belly and Mouse hit the ground a trembling mess.

"Shit," Dale whispered.

"I don't care what laws I'm breaking he's coming in the back with me. You can be chauffer," I decided, opening the back door and climbing in. Mouse jumped onto my lap and tried to curl up. I'm not a big man; he fell off twice before realising he could sit beside me.

Dale started the car and we drove off, which worked really well until I opened the window. The moment it began to descend Mouse lifted his head off my lap and replaced it with his back end so he could hang out of the window, tongue flapping, tiny ears whipping against his broad head. I vainly tried to pull him back into the car, so he shifted, flattening me against the seat and placed his paws on the sill.

"Bloody hell, you're heavy," I breathed at him.

I heard Dale chuckling from the comfort of the front seat. Fortunately it didn't take long to reach my flat. The moment we pulled up Mouse climbed off me and tried to force himself into the footwell.

"Hey, it's okay, we're going to my flat," I said.

Dale left the car and opened my door. "Here we are, sir," he said, bowing slightly.

"Har, har, I can't get the dog out," I said.

"You bring those treats?" Dale asked me.

I pulled out the bag of treats. "Mouse, we need to go home," I said, opening the bag and wafting it under his nose. He looked at me with sad brown eyes, his eyebrows dancing, the ears pulled back and down.

"Come on, Mouse, stop buggering about, I need beer," Dale announced. Mouse looked at him, looked at me and edged out of the car. I gave him a treat. It took most of the packet to convince him that we weren't going to

176

beat him to death as we walked to my front door. The moment it was open Mouse rushed in, low to the ground, found the kitchen and a corner under the table.

"How the hell did he bite me? You sure it was this dog?" I asked looking at Mouse under the table.

"It was that dog, I promise you," Dale said, helping himself to a beer from the fridge.

I retrieved the bed I'd bought, from the lounge and pushed it under the table. Mouse didn't move. I placed the water near him and the dog bowl with some nuts in it. He still didn't move.

"I'd leave him to make his own mind up," Dale said. We left the dog and spent the evening watching a movie. Dale left with a cheerful wave and I wished I knew if he wanted me to kiss him or shake his hand.

I went to bed eventually, the dog still under the table and ignoring his own bed, water and food. "Night, Mouse," I said. The dog ignored me.

I started to read yet another dog training book on my Kindle and couldn't find anything to tell me how to deal with a broken Staffy who'd chewed my face off a few weeks before.

***

I woke in the middle of the night to a sound alien in my home. I lay there, imagining the worse – they were back and about to kill me in my sleep – when I remembered I now had a dog. I rose and padded into the kitchen. Mouse, out from under the table, sat in the remains of my rubbish bin, his bowl still full of food.

"Bloody hell, Mouse," I complained. His ears flattened against his head, which sank into the shoulders and he looked up at me with miserable eyebrows.

"It's alright, mate, we'll clean it up but I would like you to eat your own food," I told him. He wagged his tail in a slightly wobbly, uncertain way. I began picking up the rubbish and Mouse moved out of my way. He picked at his food, eating slowly and watching me carefully. Once I'd cleaned the floor, I sat and took my painkillers, my arm hurting after washing the titles. Mouse came toward me and placed his chin on my leg.

"You're sorry?" I asked.

His tail swished.

"I'm sorry to, you've not had it easy," I told him.

He sighed heavily. I patted his head. "Time for bed, mate," I told him.

I rose and walked to my bedroom, the sound of four paws on my carpet coming with me.

"No, Mouse," I told him firmly.

Those eyebrows set to work and the tail wagged just a bit. The ears didn't drop, they drooped.

I sighed. "Really?"

His ears danced forward.

I caved. "Come on then."

We climbed into bed. Me under the duvet, Mouse on the duvet settling down and falling into a snoring sleep instantly.

"It's like living with the ex," I muttered, reaching for my ear plugs.

***

Mouse learned quickly. I learned even more quickly. Treats were good. Cuddles had to be on his terms. And the best thing in the world was a journey in the car. Dale came to visit us often and soon found Mouse liked going for a run. I bought him the best muzzle I could find, it being a legal necessity, and tried not to think about the looming court case. The neighbour had been forced to move but was out on bail and I remained – let's call it – vigilant.

The nights were drawing in and Dale, off duty, walked with me and Mouse around the park.

"There's that fucking queer." The voice, rough and accented in a way no one this side of the Atlantic would use, made me stop.

Dale pulled me back behind him. Mouse growled, the vibration through the lead, scaring me more than the aggressive sentiment that was all too familiar.

Three men came toward us from the darkness. One was Mouse's previous owner.

The dog growled and his weight shifted back. If he leapt I wasn't going to be able to hold the weight of him.

"Back off," Dale said. "You're on bail. You aren't supposed to be in this area as part of your bail conditions, back off." He used the key words to trigger the right response to help defuse the situation.

"That's my fucking dog," he snarled.

"No, I am the legal owner," I said. Even I heard the fear in my voice. Mouse whined and tugged on his lead. Did he want to leave me?

"I'm havin' my dog," he said, stepping forward. Dale moved to meet him. Mouse tugged hard, and the lead slipped from my sweating hand. The dog walked forward to stand beside Dale.

"Come here, Max," the man said, the command aggressive. Mouse stepped forward and growled.

"Call him, Richard. If he goes in to attack that's it, no more dog," Dale said without taking his eyes off his enemies.

"Mouse," I called.

"What? Mouse? You called my dog, Mouse? You f – "

"Mouse," I said more firmly. "Come here, we need to go home," I told my dog.

"Max, now."

"Mouse," I said.

The great head swung back toward me.

"Go on, Mouse, go back to your dad," Dale told the dog. "It's my job to protect him now, not yours."

The dog looked up at Dale, his eyes assessing the tall police man. Slowly Mouse moved back to me but the tension vibrated off him and his gaze remained on the scene in front of us.

"Get out of the park. Go home. You're on bail. One more word and I'll report you."

"One more word from you, queer pig, and I'll rip your face off."

I unhooked Mouse's muzzle, hands shaking, blood pounding and my conscience telling me this was probably dangerous and illegal. "I don't think you'll do it faster than he can," I said.

Mouse flashed his fangs. The gang stepped back as one unit.

"Until next time, piggy."

"Sure, remember to bring your army," Dale said quietly.

I breathed out and in and out and realised I was heading toward a panic attack.

Mouse leaned into my leg and licked my fingers. Dale came back to my side. "It's alright, it's over, they've gone."

"Dale..."

"I know."

"Mouse..."

A soft sentence. "I know."

"That was terrifying."

"I know."

I looked up at him and he smiled. "When are you going to kiss me, Richard?"

179

"I don't –"

"What? Fancy me?"

"You're gorgeous, Sergeant Dale Smith. Of course I want to kiss you."

"Then do it, because I'm sick of waiting and Mouse needs stable parenting," he told me.

I laughed. "He needs stable parenting."

"He does and we have to prove we are stable parents."

I smiled, stepped into the tall police body, and placed a gentle kiss on the lovely lips which kissed me back. Mouse licked my fingers and Dale's.

"See, he wants a stable family," Dale said, tickling our dog's ears.

"We are family."

The Winner Takes It All

By Sandra Staas

Author's Note: Sandra Staas has recently published on Amazon for Kindle a prequel to her upcoming debut memoir, Aventuras in Spain - a memoir of Spain in the 70's and 80's. She can be reached via her website at www.spanishinterludes.wordpress.com

The Winner Takes It All

By Sandra Staas

In 1981 my husband, small son and I were living in Urbanización El Casalot, Miami Playa, Tarragona located some 3 kilometres from the Mediterranean. It was quite common to see stray cats and dogs meandering throughout the area. They'd simply turn up on the road in front of our house and continue meandering deep into the woods. Most of them were like migrant workers who went about their own business, never staying too long in any one spot. Two dogs, however, did remain and I got to know them quite well. There was also a little kitten that I found and subsequently adopted. This is their story.

Urbanización El Casalot was a brand new development where there was still ongoing construction. Across the road from our house workmen yelled and babbled among themselves, in between peeing on the street, spitting and blowing their nose on the ground. Their transistor radio would be blaring forth loud advertisements for Galerías Preciados, condensed milk and Camel cigarettes - 'El sabor de la Aventura!'. Occasionally the workmen would burst into song, imitating Julio Iglesias singing "De Niña a Mujer" and "Hey". They were actually pretty good singers, not that I'm an expert, but Julio Iglesias himself would have been happy, I'm sure, to be listening to this open-air concert.

There was something else the workmen got up to besides hammer and bang and make lots of noise. They would play with a puppy. He looked like an Alsatian or a German Shepherd pup, based on his colouring as he frolicked about and had lots of fun playing with the workmen. They played rough with him, forcing him to the ground, preventing him from standing.

182

They'd toss left over bocadillos to him then tap his hind legs with their feet as if telling him to go away. It was difficult to see if they were actually kicking him but since the dog didn't yelp, I can only assume they never did hurt him. All seemed well until they stopped work for the day and went home. Guess what they did with the pup?

They hid him inside the house they were constructing. They basically bricked him up so that he couldn't get out. How did I know all this, you might be wondering? At night I heard him howl his little head off. He was a poor wee soul. I couldn't stand it anymore, so one Sunday when I knew the men wouldn't turn up I searched for him inside the house. The howling was coming from a corner where there were bricks stacked up. I pulled the bricks away scraping and scratching my fingers in the process. Lo and behold, there he was! He jumped up and down, his tail wagging, his tongue hanging out. He was absolutely filthy, covered in dust and cement and who knows what else.

I picked him up and took him across the road to my house and gave him a lovely bath. I fed him and offered him water. I really wanted to keep him, but reluctantly I decided that that wasn't practical. We didn't know for how long we'd continue living in the area, and anyhow, presumably he belonged to one of the workmen. I had no choice but to take him back across the road, place him in the corner and pile the bricks up around him so that he couldn't escape.

That night as I heard him whine and howl I wanted to rush over and cuddle him. I couldn't wait until morning when the workmen would be back for at least then he'd have company. On Monday morning the workmen arrived, making as much noise as a herd of elephants stomping around. I spied on them from behind the lace curtains to see if they would let the pup out. They did, thank goodness. Out he came, leaping up and down, his tail wagging furiously. He looked over at our house as if ready to visit me and have another bath, maybe some tasty food.

The workmen stared perplexedly at him, scratching their foreheads. How did the pup get so clean?! Did someone give him a bath?! I think my secret was out for the workmen turned and gazed over at our house.

"Señora loca! Crazy lady!" they called out and laughed loudly.

Thank goodness they were laughing and weren't annoyed that I had removed the pup. Maybe they really did care for the dog after all?

The other dog that I got to know I met when we first arrived in

Urbanización Casalot, when the whole place was abuzz with cheery tourists laughing and drinking until the wee small hours. People would walk about with towels around their shoulders as they made their way to the swimming pools. You could sit on your front porch and listen to live music at the restaurant just down the road. It was one long holiday all summer long.

But, come the month of October, and the place became deserted. Even the German tourists disappeared. From one day to the next, the 30th of September to the 1st of October, everything changed as the mass exodus took place. Shops and restaurants that were bustling in the summer close down for the winter. All that remained was an eerie silence as I rode my bike or went for a walk. I so looked forward to the week-ends when the Spaniards from Reus and Tarragona would come back and spend Friday and Saturday nights in their holiday homes.

There was a visitor, however, who had always stopped by every day ever since we moved to Miami Playa. It was a large friendly dog who seemed to be constantly pregnant. I had seen her many times meandering about with her pups. But then, the next time I'd see her she would be all alone. Before you knew it she would be pregnant again and then the cycle would keep on repeating itself. I would feed her, give her water and pat her on the head before she'd plod off slowly.

One cool autumn day I was walking briskly when three dogs started to follow me. I always found it best to ignore stray dogs for you never knew how they would react. I continued walking, hoping that my uneasiness wouldn't be sensed by them. They caught up with me and walked by my side. All the while I tried to keep my eyes focused on the horizon as I hastened my pace. The largest of the three dogs began to bark at me and when I glanced over it growled and snarled, showing its teeth. The other two dogs were watching closely as if to see what I would do.

I was scared. With all the tourists gone, there was nobody nearby to help me. This was before the days of cellular phones which meant I couldn't telephone anyone either. I could have been attacked, mauled even. Just then, a fourth dog turned up. Now what was going to happen?

You'll never guess what the fourth dog did.

She whacked the dog barking and growling at me with her front paw, placed her teeth on its neck and pushed it down to the ground. I was astonished. Then she whacked the other two dogs as well as if to tell them not to even considering growling and snarling.

184

Guess who the dog was? It was the friendly one who visited me each day! I believe that the three dogs may have been from one of her many litters. She was chastising them for she recognized me as the one fed her and gave her water.

It wasn't only dogs that were homeless in 1981. One day my son and I were cycling down to the neighbourhood swimming pool when what did we notice lying on a wall? It was a cute little black and white stray kitten that looked up hopefully at us as we cycled by. We just had to stop and pet him. He purred and smiled at us and seemed very tame. Well, that was us hooked. I knocked on the door of the house whose wall he was lying on in case he actually did belong to someone. Turned out the lady there was the owner of the house we were renting. She was Italian and the huge mansion she was living in for her little summer getaway residence. She told me she had been feeding the kitten pasta, but that she was returning to Italy in a few days and didn't want to take it with her.

Guess what? We kept the kitten and immediately went back home to show him to my husband who was a real cat lover.

"He's lovely!" said my husband petting the kitten. "Why don't we call him Tom Sawyer, Tom for short?"

Tom had a great life. If he wasn't outside climbing trees, he was inside lounging patiently on the back of the armchair next to the budgie cage. He was very clever was our Tom with the chubby cheeks, for he'd pretend to be asleep any time you'd walk by. Then, when he thought nobody would notice, he'd sit up straight and whack the budgie cage with his paw. If you turned round to scold him, he'd quickly crouch down and pretend once again to be asleep. He was simply fascinated by the budgie!

Our budgie, Peter Pan, felt so secure in his cage that he just literally stood his ground and basically ignored the cat. In fact, I think Peter Pan quite liked the cage swinging back and forth each time Tom Sawyer swiped it with his paw. He'd whistle loudly and talk to the budgie he saw in the little mirror hanging in his cage. Maybe there was a mutual understanding between the cat and the bird.

This may sound like domestic bliss reigned in Urbanización Casalot, Miami Playa. But it wasn't all sugar and spice.

One evening, I was sitting on the front porch listening to the live music coming from the German night club across the road. The group was playing "The Winner Takes it All" and I tried to figure out the nationality of the

185

singers. Could be German? Could be Swedish? Or Spanish? Actually, no matter where they came from they were quite good and I'm sure Abba would have been pleased with their performance. The neighbours, two doors down, were dancing in the road. They waved their arms high in the sky and snapped their fingers as if they were dancing some Catalan version of Sevillanas or of the Birdie Dance. It was a delightful evening now that the sun was no longer a blazing cannonball and I marvelled at how lucky I was to be in Spain, just three kilometers from the Mediterranean Sea. I sipped on my ice cold Brandy Alexander and sighed with contentment.

In the background I discerned a high pitched noise. What could it be? Perhaps a baby crying? The live music was thumping away and people were shrieking with laughter. I wondered if laughter sounds the same in every language? Is there such a thing as German laughter, British laughter, American laughter, etc.?

I tried to ignore the sounds from the German night club and focus on the strange wailing noise that seems to be emanating to my left, at the side of the house, next to a bush. When the music stopped I immediately realised that it was not a baby crying, after all. It was a cat miaowing at the top of its lungs. It must be Tom Sawyer! Where was he? And why was he so upset?

I walked over towards the bushes. There he was. His back was up and when he saw me he started to hiss. What could be wrong with him? Normally, he was very docile. From the other side of the bush a big fat cat appeared, all the while wailing and howling. It too had its back up. He was intent on invading Tom's territory and a cat fight was about to erupt! What to do? Tom was not yet fully grown, and going by the size of the other cat, it could easily have devoured poor old Tom.

"Go away! At once!" I ordered the other cat and clapped my hands.

Did this work? Nope. Guess what happened next! Tom Sawyer turned round to face me and miaowed long and sharp at me.

"Tom. Tom. Come here." I bent down to pick him up. He held his ground and hissed at me, his back even higher up than before. He was reprimanding me, telling me to leave, for this was his battle and he could handle it.

Now, I'm good at taking hints. Absolutely. I took a few steps backwards. Guess what Tom did? He marched over to me, all the while miaowing his head off as if telling me to get lost and for me to stop interfering. At the same time the big fat cat was wailing louder as he approached Tom who turned around and wailed even louder than the fat cat.

I so wished I had a bucket of water.

Can you imagine a time when fighting is eradicated? When threats are just music ringing out in the evening air, when wars and battles silently dissipate midst the bushes and borders. All that we need is a bucket of water to toss on the cries of both sides. It has to be so simple.

I went back on the front porch and tried not to think about Tom Sawyer and his first encounter with a raging fat feline. I knew enough about cats to realise that territory is important to them and that it's instinct to protect it at all costs. I just hoped he wouldn't get hurt.

The cat fight began. Based on the racket and the scuffling it certainly sounded like a major battle. Fortunately, the band started playing again drowning out the noise a little with their rendition of Captain and Tennile's "Do That To Me One More Time". Something told me that neither cat would be singing along with these lyrics.

I resisted the temptation to get a broom and shoo the fat cat away. If Tom had wanted me to help him he wouldn't have yelled at me so much. If he were to win the fight due to my getting involved then what self-respect could he possibly ever have? He obviously felt he could handle the situation, don't you think?

There was a silence by the bushes. I was relieved that the fight, short and to the point was over. But now what? I hesitated as I was too scared to investigate lest Tom be lying on the ground bleeding. Maybe I should have got rid of the fat cat? Maybe Tom was just too wee to be fighting that great big lump of a cat?

"Miaow!" Tom pranced over to me. "Miaow!" He sounded pleased with himself, and quite a happy defender of his territory.

"Are you okay? Are you hurt?" I examined him carefully, relieved that he was talking to me in his usual cheerful way. He did seem perfectly fine. I noticed the fat cat zooming down the road, whizzing past the merry neighbours dancing in the street.

Tom Sawyer with the chubby cheeks walked up and down and round and round purring as he brushed against my leg. Then stared up at me as if to say, "See? I won."

What A Lucky Little Lad

By Jonathan Fogell

What A Lucky Little Lad

By Jonathan Fogell

Neither Dot nor Jonathan was accustomed to watching the TV during the day. Despite being retired from their professions, they had little time or appetite for day-time TV either in French or in English. It was Saturday 5 July 2014. On the TV was the Grand Depart of Le Tour de France, and it was starting from Leeds, of all places. That afternoon Dot and Jonathan sat watching on the TV, the sun soaked northern English setting contrasted with their rain soaked quartier in the South of France

They lived in Clairac, a village halfway between Bordeaux and Toulouse. It is a beautiful village but it has seen better days. It was once a bustling little commercial centre that had built a small fortune on tobacco, prunes and animal feeds but the heady days were over. The cigarette factory in nearby Tonneins had closed, and farming offered so few low paid jobs that times were hard.

Still the folk of Clairac knew how to fete during the late spring and summer months. They put on a magnificent firework display every July 14, Bastille Day. Several weeks before then, is the national 'Fete de Musique', where musicians busk in the streets for local people and visitors who stroll around to the strains of everything from punk to baroque music. The quality of the musicianship is astounding

"Would you be willing to do a set on the stage in the Place de Liberté"? The Mayor asked Rory, a musician friend of Jonathan. "I'd love to replied Rory, how much do you pay?" Rory was unfamiliar with the tradition of the Fete de Musique. "Oh there is no fee, musicians give their time for free", the Mayor replied jovially. "OK" replied Rory, "and when with the next fete de mason be? I need a wall building and I'd like it done for free." The Mayor

189

looked quizzically at Rory and there followed a moment of dead air. "OK, I'm joking, I'll do it" Rory said, and the Mayor looked bemused, gave a small Gallic shrug, and said, "Ah bon". Roughly translated that meant, "Whatever".

On the night of the June 21, Dot and Jonathan took a walk around the centre of Clairac and listened to the music playing in eight different locations. As they arrived in the Place de Liberté, they saw Rory on the stage. He was playing the Charlie Mingus dedication to Lester Young, 'Goodbye Porkpie Hat', on pan pipes. Jonathan always found the sound of the pan pipes to be somewhat incongruous with Smooth Jazz, but that is what Rory played, and the Mayor seemed to like it. They sat down on a wall close to the stage and Liyung, Rory's wife came wandering along and stopped to talk with them. Liyung had left Rory to live in Bordeaux, but she came back with Timoté, their son, to see his dad every couple of weeks.

Liyung stopped and chatted with Jonathan and Dot. She is a thirty-something Chinese girl who could chat very comfortably in English despite never having set foot in any English speaking country. She also spoke French like a native. After a while Liyung asked "Do you know anybody selling or giving away a kitten?" Jonathan and Dot thought hard. Off hand, they did not know anyone wanting to find a home for a kitten, but they promised that they would ask around on Liyung's behalf. It seemed an odd thing to ask in the middle of a conversation about how her house move went, and was Timoty getting on well in his new school? Her enquiry was, however, logical because they had been troubled by mice in their new place, and the best way to scare off mice, was to have a cat occupying the house. Liyung's decision to look for a kitten had delighted Timoté.

Two weeks after their natter with Liyung, Dot and Jonathan had all but forgotten her request. They watched the start of the Tour de France and then saw the riders on the Pennine climb sections near Harrogate. They were amazed at the beautiful sunny weather in the North of England. The crowds had come out making a scene for the race organizers that could have been Nice or Montpelier or indeed almost anywhere but Leeds. In Clairac, the rain was drying up and it looked like it would become a hot day there too.

By the evening Dot and Jonathan had promenaded Myrtille, the collie/spaniel cross, and Remy, the pure race border collie. They had taken them through the local kiwi orchards and down to the River Lot for a cooling swim and stick chase. Having had their appetites whetted for cycling, Dot and Jonathan decided to go on a bike ride to cool off.

All along the river to the end of the low road to Castelmoron, the route was calm. They passed the fields and plastic tunnels full of strawberries, on past the tumbledown farmhouse and along to the place where, many years ago, a railway line crossed the river Lot as it weaved its way down to Aiguillon to the confluence with the Garonne. That is where the Lot ceased to be a mere riviere and became a fleuve that flowed out past Bordeaux and out to the Bay of Biscay. Dot and Jonathan rested a while at the furthest point of their ride before turning round and retracing their route back home.

"Dot suddenly said "Shall we go a little further? We could go over the bridge through Lafitte and back along the road at the other side". It was still light and the warm gentle evening breeze made cycling effortless. "Why not?" Jonathan replied and he turned his bike around to continue and double their 5km ride. They traversed the old suspension bridge and headed over to Laffite and then returned back home again along the road that hugged the river. They were cycling along the main road and the River Lot flowed gently alongside. They were about two hundred metres from the sign announcing that one had reached Clairac. Suddenly they heard a loud insistent 'meow' sound. "Oh dear, that sounds like a cat in trouble", Dot and Jonathan said in unison.

They rode past the plaintive cries but stopped twenty metres further along and got off their bikes. Jonathan said "I'm going to see what it is." Dot sounded a word of caution. "If it's a kitten or an injured cat you will not be able to leave it there." Jonathan had past the point of no return. As he retraced his steps the cries were growing ever more insistent. He went over to the hedge approximately where the sound was coming from. "Chum on" he said gently, using the same words and tone he would use with Yoda, their own sphinx cat. She came to such tones whenever she felt like it. "Chum on little one" he said and then followed up with.... ch ch ch sounds.

The thick luscious grass started to shake and move. Out came a very tiny ginger kitten that was about 8 weeks old. What could have happened to this kitten? It was too far away from any house to have wandered away. It knew humans and it knew they might quell its hunger pangs. Not everybody wants a cat especially in country areas in France and especially at the start of the holiday season. The first week in July is a very dangerous time for too many domestic pets. There are those who have a cat may not want another and so the kittens become a problem. Not everyone is kind to animals. Some people sadly throw cats in rivers ditches to try to get rid of them. So Dot and Jonathan assumed that this is what may have happened to this little cat.

Dot was right. They could not leave this noisy little fluff ball there. She had pannier bags on her bike so she placed the kitten in one of them and zipped it shut. The kitten did not seem unduly bothered about this. He must have been confident his luck had changed and, even though he was zipped into a pitch black bag he was sure things were going to turn out OK, and they were. It took us 5 minutes to cycle back home. All along the road the kitten reminded them that sooner or later he would need to be let out of the bag Meow. Meow... MEOW... MEOW....! went Dot's pannier bag as they cycled home.

When they reached home they lifted him out of the bag. He made no attempt to struggle. He had no claws at the ready just in case. He looked well and he was flea free. "I wonder if he is hungry." Jonathan said and he went to get a bowl of Yoda's grub. Was he hungry? Man, was he hungry? He dived into the food like a very very hungry kitten. Dot put him in Yoda's cat box with his bowl of food and he devoured it in record time. They then put him into a little corridor that could be isolated for a while from Yoda, Myrtille and Remy who may have been none too happy about this noisy hungry thing invading their territory.

The little kitten settled into his spacious accommodation with en-suite litter tray, bowl of fresh water, crispy crunchy cat croquets and a comfortable soft platform to sleep on safely. During the night Jonathan was awoken by a huge storm with lots of thunder and lightning and a cloudburst that went on for hours. He thought of that little kitten out there on the verge next to the river. He had had a lucky escape. He would have been scared and in danger of being washed down the riverbank and off with the ever faster flowing Lot. "He was not lucky to be abandoned but, in the circumstances, He's a lucky lad", Jonathan said to himself as he drifted back to sleep.

The next morning the kitten was carefully introduced to Myrtille and Remy. Myrtille was a little more reticent than Remy who reacted with more than his usual indifference. Indeed it would be fair to say that Remy could not have given one, let alone two hoots, about the cat. It was not a stick and it was not a ball and it could not be eaten and so it was of no consequence whatsoever (welcome to the Border Collie world). Mrytille did not look too happy until towards the end of the first day. She then wanted to lick the kitten all over as often as she could. At home with small animals, Myrtille is a very gentle dog. Out in the fields she is a hunter although not a very successful one. How lucky was that to end up in the house of a friendly licking dog? Yoda let out a large hiss at the sight of the little ginger interloper and then turned and retreated to her boudoir. I think the hiss meant something like "I'll be back".

Dot and Jonathan already had three animals and did not want another. They were just beginning to face up to the fact that they may have to keep this new lodger when they remembered Liyung's demand. Five minutes after Dot had said "What about Liyung?" by grace of Facebook, she had sent a message with a photo of the kitten and got a reply. Liyung said emphatically "we would love to have him and from now on can you call him Ginger". Timoté let out a squeal and punched the air as his mum composed her response. She told Jonathan and Dot that she would pick him up the following Saturday. How lucky was this little abandoned kitten?

So during the week all their animals, even Yoda, watched this tiny kitten become braver and friendlier with them. After some sniffs of his tail and nose, Yoda started playing with him. Dot and Jonathan had great fun watching it all. So only after 4 days Ginger had settled in as if he had always lived there and all thoughts of those lonely few hours on the river bank had gone. He even started stealing Myrtille's dinner. How cheeky can a little kitten be …? Even more bizarre was that Myrtille sat and waited patiently for Ginger to eat his fill, before starting her dinner of whatever else was left. I would call that seriously lucky; to live with a dog like that.

Jonathan and Dot gave Ginger a collar with a bell. The bells helped them know where the cats were in the house. When there was silence they would think…! Oh dear where are they, and worse still what are they up to?

Ginger is certainly a plucky kitten who has survived being thrown away. He once was lost but then he was found. You could write a song about that entitled 'Amazing Luck'. But Ginger made much of his own luck with his very affectionate cuddling and and purrrrings. He would sit on Dot's lap purring when she was typing on the computer. When he looked up, with his big doe eyes, it didn't matter what mischief he had been involved in, Dot and Jonathan immediately started to smile and think kind thoughts.

Ginger played with a small soft play mouse. He would get his little claws caught in the fabric. He would then try to throw it away. After several violent thrusts the mouse would fly from his claws and Ginger would then run very fast to chase it again. Yoda had taken to stalking Ginger. She watched him intently and then started doing the same daft things. Dot and Jonathan had many chuckles watching the pair play.

After a period if intensive play, Ginger would conk out fast asleep. He did not need to retreat to his sleeping tower. He used the sofa, the bean bag the carpet, Myrtille's bed and from time to time even Remy's bed. He settled into a similar pattern of sleep as Yoda although never on the same cushion. Yoda and Ginger loved to snuggle but never with each other. Luckily for Ginger, when Yoda was snuggling up to a human, there was always another one spare for him to snuggle up to. As for Jonathan and Dot they began to get quite used to having his and hers purr pots.

So it was with a little sadness that Dot and Jonathan welcomed Timoté and Liyung at the end of the week. They had come over from Bordeaux to take Ginger to live with them. They took him away to live in their chic little house in the Bordeaux suburbs. He would play with toys and Timoté and to snuggle up to his new humans. One week ago he was a lost and frightened kitten crying in the grass verge between a main road and a river. He had a few hours to go before the biggest storm of the year would arrive and he spotted Jonathan and Dot. Today he is in a new home with Timoté and Liyung. Yoda, Mrytille and Remy had helped that little frightened kitten to learn new things.

Liyung sent Dot and Jonathan a picture of Ginger at the end of his first day in his new home. He was curled up next to his new best mate Timoté. The two of them were exhausted after a good play together. When Jonathan looked at the image he turned to Dot and said "I'd say they are a lucky pair of lads wouldn't you?

What In The Sam Hill...

By Tina Mattern

What In The Sam Hill...

By Tina Mattern

"No more cats!" That's what my husband, Fred, told the kids and me. "Three cats are more than enough." My daughter, Summer, and I just looked at each other and grinned. Yeah... like you can *ever* have too many cats! Then again, we weren't planning on adding any new members to our fur family, so the issue didn't seem worth debating. But that was before Sam came on the scene.

My friend, Denise and I had stopped for dinner at a country-western pub on the outskirts of Portland, and on our way in a black and white cat came flying past to perch on the hood of a nearby car.

What can I say? I'm a sucker for cats and this one was oozing with "doncha want to pet me?" charm. So I did. I walked over and scratched him behind the ears. The purr kicked into high gear and he leaned heavily against my fingers.

I wondered where he came from; there were no houses nearby, just an empty field on one side and a tree farm on the other." I picked him up and gave him a warm snuggle. The cat burrowed his face into my neck in obvious ecstasy. "It's a shame he's so unfriendly," I laughed. I put him down on the sidewalk and Denise and I went inside.

During dinner, I found myself thinking about the little guy outside in the cold, obviously hungry for attention. So, I asked the waitress if she knew anything about the young cat in the parking lot. She told us that someone had abandoned the mother and her four kittens in the field next door. The restaurant staff had fed and looked after them until the kittens were weaned and then one by one, they'd been adopted by either the employees or customers. "One of the cooks even took the mom cat home. The one outside is the only one left. Sweet, isn't he?"

I nodded and looked helplessly at Denise. She grinned, "Uh-oh. Looks like someone's going to be a four-cat family!"

"It's late though," I said, "He's probably long gone by now."

He wasn't. He was sitting on the hood of another car when we came out. If cats could smile, he was smiling his face off and we could hear him purring from 6 feet away. I scooped him up, said goodnight to Denise and headed for my van. Putting him on the passenger seat, I belted myself in and prepared for him to freak out when I started the car. He didn't. He stretched languidly across the seat with his front paws curled beneath him and looked expectantly at me. His expression was clear. "Home, James!"

When we got to the house, I gathered the cat from his comfy position and wrapped him in my coat. As I walked into the family room where the gang was watching TV, Aaron, our son, looked up and seeing a tail dangling from beneath my jacket, said, "Hey, what in the Sam Hill is that under your coat?" giving my hitch-hiker the perfect name.

"It's our new kitty—Sam Hill!" I announced, opening my coat with a flourish and hoping Sam's cuteness would win Fred over.

It did. Sam grinned his irresistible cat grin, Fred groaned and muttered but before the evening was over, he, along with the kids, became a Sam fan. The other cats hissed at him once or twice but then, like the rest of us, fell under his spell. The kitty without a home had found a family.

The first order of business on Sam's agenda was to establish his number one rule: No closed doors! He promptly set about teaching himself to open said doors, which, fortunately for him, were equipped with latch-type handles. Within a few weeks, he had set off the burglar alarm in the house at least three times and shocked unsuspecting guests who were using the bathroom. The laundry room, off the TV room, was where we kept the litter box, but when the dryer was running, it was hard to hear the television, so we always closed the door; Sam didn't approve—he'd open it. We'd close it, etcetera. It was through this little idiosyncrasy that we discovered another aspect of our endlessly entertaining boy: he was apparently psychic. When one of the other cats found the door to the laundry room closed, they would sit, staring patiently at the portal until, only minutes later, Sam, from wherever he had been sleeping in the house, would come and open the door for them. Eventually though, this fascinating facet of Sam's personality wore thin and Fred finally put his foot down: "I'm either going to put a metal plate on the door and make that cat wear a magnet on his rear end or..." He changed the handles to regular doorknobs. Sam was seriously bummed, both for himself and his brothers-in-fur.

All creatures, two-legged or four, were friends, in Sammy's book. People were great, cats were cool, and dogs were dandy. He didn't even bat a whisker when I brought home a dwarf rabbit named Bunny Jean. Before a week was out, they were best buddies, chasing each other around the family room. We had a sheepskin rug in front of the fireplace—Sam would dive under it, every part of him covered except his nose—then wait patiently until Bunny Jean came hopping by. When he pounced, the two would roll around on the carpet, wrestle and play hide and seek until one or the other finally collapsed into a nap. They were infinitely more captivating than most of the shows available on television.

Every day, it seemed, we would discover a new component to our Sam's repertoire of personality quirks. One afternoon when I was working around the house, I heard Sam meowing loudly. He rarely did this so when it continued for quite some time I got a little concerned and went to see what was going on. Following his voice, I found him in the kitchen, sitting on the floor, looking intently up at, and having a heartfelt conversation with...the oven. He glanced over at me then went on chatting. When he was finished with his tête-à-tête, he smoothed a whisker and headed to the sofa for a nap. Off and on after that, I would find him in the living room having the same dialogue with the drapes. He was a nut, but never boring.

Samuel William Hill was cherished by our family for nine wonderful years. These days though, he's hanging out in heaven, keeping the angels amused, opening doors for them I'm sure, and waiting for his family to come home.

A Day In The Life Of Phoebe

By Sue Evans

Author's note - the story is based on my life-long study of the cats I have owned. Phoebe is my current cat (I have two) and is seven years old. Bad Harry is, as the story relates, the neighbour's cat and the two of them do call for one another and go hunting together. We live in the country and so we are often finding their gifts in the house. Photographs could be provided!

A Day In The Life Of Phoebe

By Sue Evans

Every night I have to go through the same routine. I've discussed the problem with Bad Harry who lives at number four and apparently his mum and dad leave the bedroom door open. But not mine. Bad Harry said that they are probably not very bright; they obviously love me and so I mustn't take it personally. I don't know why they close the door at night but leave it open during the day. Anyway, every pink morning time, I have to keep scratching and shouting until they let me in. Mum is always so sleepy but I let her stroke me before snuggling down in the lovely, warm bed. This is the best time of the sky and eventually I curl up in a tight ball in the bendy bit of her knees.

Not long after, that awful tick-tocky box makes that piercing sound that hurts my ears. It used to frighten me so much at one time that I used to run out of the room but I'm used to it now. Goodness only knows why they have it. It wakes them up when they are asleep- I can think of nothing worse- and it always makes them groan. Then dad stops the noise by bashing it with his hand which usually means that it falls onto the floor. Then they both lie perfectly still for a couple of minutes before getting up: from nice cosy silence to manic dashing and fussing. What a palaver! All this silliness just to go mousing and rabbiting. Why they don't go out at night, when mouses and rabbits are easy to catch? Bad Harry and I think they are slightly mad – which is a shame because, really, they are very nice people.

Another thing we don't understand is why, when we bring them tasty morsels, they throw them in the bin! Lovely, tasty, fresh food. How ungrateful! Yet, when they return from a day's hunting, they have chopped up the meat, coated it in the most revolting jelly or gravy, removed the bones which are delicious and keep our teeth clean, and then- can you believe it – shoved it all in smelly tins!! Often it makes us feel ill! After all, as Bad Harry says, you never see them eating it do you? And then, if that isn't enough, when their awful food has made us poorly, they shove a white thing down our throats! It tastes disgusting and so we spit it out and run off but that acts as a *cat*alyst for what can only be called abusive behaviour. They chase us round and round, shouting and frightening us half to death until they catch us. Holding us down, they force open our mouths until we have no choice but to swallow the thing. How undignified. Bad Harry and I frequently go on hunger strike but they never learn.

Anyway, back to the morning ritual. Once they've finally got up it's best to get out of their way. They are particularly clumsy, falling over me when I brush past their legs. Once in the bathroom where they make some very funny noises while drinking out of the toilet, I go downstairs to sit on top of the window-sill which has a metal thing underneath which gets really warm. I love it. The trouble is it doesn't stay warm for long. Still, by the time it goes cold, mum and dad have left and so I go upstairs again, back to bed and curl up for a light- sky nap.

It is very cold today. I make a nice cosy nest for myself by patting down the bed cover until it is like a little wall around me. No-one can get me then. I curl my tail right round my face to keep out any draughts and then go fast asleep.

Suddenly I hear a noise; someone is downstairs. Must be mum. She comes home first. I get up and stretch. Today has gone very quickly. I must have slept for a long time. I go downstairs to say hello- I know my manners - when I see someone else there. A dad I don't know. He seems alright though and says, "Hello Kitty, Kitty," to me. I tell him my name isn't Kitty and ask him why is he there but he isn't really listening. He goes upstairs and I follow him. He goes into the bedroom and takes off the pillow cases. How strange! Perhaps he's going to wash them. Mum does that every week. I like the bed when it's been cleaned. In fact there's nothing I like more than sitting on the clean washing, especially when it's been raining outside and I'm wet, muddy and cold.

The strange dad then starts to do odd things. He tips the contents of the bedside drawers and jewellery boxes into the pillow cases. He gives me a stroke and I purr, asking him politely what he is doing but he seems in a hurry and soon makes his way downstairs. I decide to go and see Bad Harry. He'll know who he is. Bad Harry knows everything.

I go through Harry's cat door and as usual, he's asleep on the settee. I call him and he soon wakes up. He's pleased to see me but as usual he tries to jump on my back which I don't like at all. Very rude! I always have to hiss at him and give him a slap before he stops. He tells me he's sorry but I don't believe him. If he was really sorry he wouldn't do it again would he? I then tell him about the new dad who is at our house. Bad Harry knows all about people like him. One of his dad's (he's had many) was one. He explained all about what he was doing; how people like him take things from one home and bring them back to their home. Like Robin Hood."

I've never heard of Robin Hood but I don't tell Bad Harry that. He'd only think I was thick.

Bad Harry then starts to laugh. "You'll never guess what they call dads like that?"

"No," I say. "I only went to the local Secondary Mog whereas you went to the Acatamy." It's a sore point.

Bad Harry ignores me and starts to titter. "They call them, wait for it...*cat burglars*," and he starts to laugh so much that he rolls around on the floor.

I look at Bad Harry in disdain. "That's just plain silly and I don't believe you," I say, growling a little to show how irritated I am.

"No, it's true. My dad cat burglar often came home with pillow cases full of things. Then he put them in bags and went out. When he came back he didn't have the things any more but he did have lots of white powdery stuff which he sniffed. It always made him happy. I don't know why. I had a sniff, but it was horrible, worse than our cat food."

"Did you?" I asked, full of admiration. Bad Harry is very brave and will try anything.

"Then one night," Harry continues, "It was dark and dad was in bed. I'd just got back from hunting and curled up on the bed. Suddenly, I heard this high-pitched noise that really hurt my ears -it was really loud and getting louder. Then these cars with flashing lights stopped outside our house. Dad jumped out of bed quicker than I've ever seen him and climbed out of the bedroom window. But the flashy- light people broke the door down and found him. He tried to run away over the roofs but he fell down and they got him. The flashy- light people put him in their car and I never saw him again."

Bad Harry stopped talking, licked his paw and wiped his face. He always did that when he was upset.

"It was a tough time for me then, Phoebe, I can tell you. I had to get all my own food which, as you well know, isn't always easy especially in the winter, and the house was always icy cold. I could never get warm. At last a lady saw me and took me to the... well... you know where."

"Not the..." I hesitated, hardly daring to say it. "Not the V.E.T.S!!!"

"Yes."

We were both quiet for a while.

"What happened then?" I whispered.

Bad Harry gave me a long look. "What always happens at the... you know where. They jabbed me with needles, forced vile things down my mouth which made me gag, and if that wasn't bad enough, rammed a cold stick up my bottom. I could barely contain myself I can tell you. I gave one of them a right swipe with my paw."

I gasped in horror. What a *cat*astrophe!

"Anyway, as it happens, it turned out alright after that. At least it was warm at the... you know where... and they gave me some food and biscuits. The following day these people took me away in their car to a garden where they put me in a wooden cage with wire windows. There were other cats there too. Most of them were very nice and we got talking. Some of them had had terrible things happen to them. I can't bare thinking about it." Bad Harry licked his paw and wiped his face before continuing, "Our new mum and dad fed us and talked to us and the mom used to brush my long hair – heaven. I remember that at first it really hurt and she had to cut a lot of it off. But it grew back and then I loved being brushed. Then, one day, the mum and dad who look after me now brought me here. And the rest, as they say, is history." I lick his nose to show him how much I enjoyed the story and then we made our way to the kitchen to drink some milk.

After we cleaned ourselves, Bad Harry went back to the settee and before I even had time to chase my tail, he's snoring. I love Bad Harry and he is my best friend but he is one lazy cat!

As I trotted home I remembered other things Bad Harry had told me about his previous dad; how he used to kick and smack him, not feed him for days and how his coat used to hurt because it was so tangled and knotty. My mum and dad would never do that. I guess I've trained them well.

The house was empty when I got back but what a mess, things

everywhere. Mum and dad wouldn't like that! The cat burglar had also left the back door open which made the house even colder. How rude! I ran upstairs to enjoy my afternoon constitutional and guess what? He'd left all sorts of things over the bed, just where I go to sleep! What a cheek.

At last Mum came home. She called me as usual to give her a fuss, but then she stopped and I heard her gasp and start to race around muttering. I then heard her talk into that plastic thing she puts next to her ear. She sounded really upset and her voice was funny. When she ran upstairs and saw me on the bed, she started to cry. She usually smiles when she sees me and so I put two and two together and realised that the cat burglar had upset her. I told her all about what had happened but she ignored me completely. Dad was soon home and then those people with the flashy lights that Bad Harry had told me about came. Oh no!! They were going to take my mum and dad away! I would be left to die!

I was so scared that when mum sat on my chair – I let her borrow it in the evenings- I jumped on her lap and made a very tight ball so that she could not move without taking me with her. The flashy- light people talked and talked and mom and dad talked and talked. Eventually the flashy- light people went to the door and dad showed them out. What a relief! They did not take mum or dad with them! Mom started to stroke me very roughly but I let her because I could tell she was upset. When they went to bed, for the first time ever, they left the door open and so I joined them. It's good to know that I'm so comforting to them in their hour of need. However when it was dark black sky, I just couldn't stay in any more. I get this fidgety feeling that makes me go out. Bad Harry gets it too. There were mice to hunt and possibly rabbits to eat and it's all so exciting!

Harry was already outside, waiting for me, to hunt the fields together. I told him about the flashy-light people but that they hadn't taken mom or dad away. "That's alright then," he said and gave my head a lick. He is such a kind friend.

The field was full of noises and it was fun to compare and identify them. We saw a few rats but we didn't try and get them. They have nasty sharp teeth and are no fun at all. Foxy ran past quickly and said "hello." Stuart the owl hooted at us. We looked at one another, acknowledging that we had competition. Stuart was an expert mouse-catcher.

At last we felt vibrations and smelled the biscuit smell – the sign of mouses and their holes. In fact I just missed catching one. It didn't bother us.

They always come out in the end. We positioned ourselves either side of the hole and waited and waited.

Mum was telling the kids not to go out but one, called Alice, was behaving very badly and started to squeak loudly, saying that she was never allowed out and it wasn't fair!! Mum said that she was going out too often, that her boyfriend Sid was a bad influence and that she was grounded.

Me and Bad Harry could tell that as soon as her mum's back was turned, Alice would run out and then we'd get her. We'd probably get Sid as well. They're such good fun when you do catch them, especially the naughty ones. They put up a bit of a fight and carry on squeaking even when you throw them up in the air. Sometimes they even play dead. Bad Harry dozed a bit and so I was on sentry duty. We work well together.

A long time passed and Bad Harry woke up. Just as he opened his eyes, he saw a tiny paw emerge from the hole. Alice's no doubt. Now Harry has just passed his Grade 6 Pouncing Examination and before you could say Jack Rabbit, he dragged all of naughty Alice out. We heard mum squeak, "Serves you right my girl. That'll teach you!"

Alice was most obliging, squeaking loudly when we threw her into the air and even playing dead a couple of times. Then she went all limp and this time we knew she was finished. I ate the head and Bad Harry the body. Delicious. Much, much better than the stuff in tins.

Making our way home, Bad Harry asked me to marry him again. I told him that although I really liked him, I only ever thought of him as a brother. I wish I could feel differently about him but I can't.

Besides a new Tortoise Shell has moved in next to us whose absolutely gorgeous. He introduced himself yesterday. He's called Scarface – handsome and dangerous – and gave me a cheeky wink! Then he washed his entire body in front of me. You could tell he went to the gym. Besides – and I'd never tell Bad Harry this – I just don't fancy male long-haired cats – a bit effeminate if you ask me.

Sky time was pale pink by the time we got home and after giving Bad Harry a quick lick goodnight, I ran upstairs and straight onto the bed. Time for a thorough clean – some mouse bits and pieces were round my mouth and face. I'd even got some on my tail. Then sleep...

A few sky-colour changes later, tick-tock screeched and mum and dad got up for hunting again. Before they finally got out of bed, I gave them both long licks to show how much I loved them.

207

Epilogue

The following day everything was back to normal. The cat burglar didn't come back – nor did the people with the flashy lights. Mum and dad went hunting again and when they came home they were very pleased to see me. That night I went out by myself. I deliberately didn't wait for Bad Harry. I didn't want to share my catch with him. I had other plans. It took me all night but finally I caught, not one, but two mice! I dearly wanted to eat them but I carefully brought them home, one at a time, and took them lovingly through the cat door leaving them at the bottom of the stairs. What a lovely surprise for mum and dad.

Oh, just one last thing before I go – the magnificent Scarface has just asked me out! I'm so glad mum and dad have just bought me a new collar.

R a f a

By Pauline Rodgers

Rafa

By Pauline Rodgers

I had not been living in Spain for long years ago and my mother was visiting. We decided to go to Malaga for the day. We took the bus to avoid parking problems.

We had a lovely day and around five went to catch the bus back to Marbella. It was very busy, crowds of people to-ing and fro-ing when we saw a little dog obviously lost and worried, frantically looking at all the crowds as if trying to see someone. We stopped and spoke to him. He was holding his paw up, obviously injured and what little hair he had left someone had thrown green paint onto him. Then an old Spanish lady in black, stooped, with a walking stick stopped and bent towards the dog. She said, "perro pobre, perro pobre."

Mum and I had to catch the bus so we left. Well what a night we had thinking about the little dog so the next day we went back in the car. We went to the same area but he wasn't there. We looked and looked and were just about to leave after a good few hours. We were near the disused train station where there was a wall with arches going into an old car park. Suddenly we saw the old lady in black going through one of the arches and following her was the little dog. We ran after them and there was the dog sitting in the middle of the car park but no old lady yet there was no other way out. Anyway we managed to entice the dog with a croissant we had bought, swiftly tying a belt round his neck and carrying him to my car. We took him to the vet who said he was about one or two years old and had fleas, the mange and an injured leg. All resolvable. So I adopted Rafael Jose, Rafa for short.

I said to my mum that evening after we had bathed him and fed him, that it was strange that the old Spanish lady had stroked him the first time we saw him and then was with him again when we found him. My mum said "What old lady. I didn't see an old lady either of those times. He was alone."

He is now sixteen and not too well but he keeps going. He's been a loyal, funny, yappy little dog, loved and respected by all the family. His eyes light up still when he sees me. I know he trusts the family implicitly. At first he had many issues and fears, for instance, he had a fear of motorway bridges. Would not walk over them. However he overcame all that years ago and is a brave loving friend who's brought joy to us all.

I hope when he goes off to doggy heaven, his old lady friend will be waiting to look after him there. I really hope so.

Beloved Pets Moving On To The Spirit World

By Alison Wynne-Ryder (The Quirky Medium)

A pet is a part of the family, they ask for nothing other than to be fed, watered & loved. They are content wherever they live, as long as it's with you. They don't need fancy things, just to know that their unconditional love for you is reciprocated. You can tell them anything, & they won't spread rumours (they can keep a secret) & they don't judge. I wrote this piece to help anyone who has lost a pet or is about to - because I know firsthand, that their love never dies as they journey from this world to the next. Alison Wynne-Ryder - Co-host on the TV *Show Rescue Mediums, Clairvoyant Medium* and author of the bestselling book *The Quirky Medium.*

@rescuemediumali

Beloved Pets Moving On To The Spirit World

By Alison Wynne-Ryder (The Quirky Medium)

When I met John (who is now my husband) I eventually moved into his house with 'my baggage'! - My daughter Lauren, my cat Topsy and dog Jet. Lauren loved her new home and Topsy and Jet had settled too. This tail (sorry I couldn't resist!) is a lovely memory I would like to share about both of them.

After a couple of years living in the house we decided to get a puppy as a companion for Jet. We chose a female black Labrador as our new addition to the family and we called her Libby. She is one of the most lovable and gentle creatures I have ever had the privilege of meeting and even our cat Topsy, who wasn't one for cuddles or affection, absolutely loved Libby. She used to rub her head on Libby's big head every morning as a greeting and often curled up with her at night.

Over time I noticed that Topsy, who was now around fifteen years old, was getting very thin and frail. She was a very old lady, but she was eating and drinking and was happy, with her tail always in the air. Never a cat that you could pick up, she remained aloof with everyone apart from me. There was a total connection without words, a sort of telepathy that went on between us that, to be honest, neither my husband nor my daughter could understand. The day came when spirit told me she would be 'taken over the rainbow bridge'. I rang in to work and told them I wouldn't be in as my cat would be leaving this mortal world and luckily they knew me well. When my husband came down in his police uniform I still had my dressing gown on. He asked why I wasn't ready for work so I told him I wasn't going in as Topsy was going over to the rainbow bridge. He asked how I knew and I said

I just did; although he stood there looking incredulous he knew better than to argue with me so he went off to work.

Not long after he had gone, Topsy lay down by the radiator in our living room. She felt cold so I put a soft blanket over her and knelt down beside her. She looked at me and raised her paws at me. I was so upset at losing my friend of fifteen years and asked the angels to help me. All of a sudden I felt a warm breeze around me and a sense of calm. I looked at Topsy who had laid her head down but was still looking at me and I talked to her softly giving her some Reiki as the angels took her gentle soul away. I saw glittery lights like stars over her body, and eventually she was gone. I was absolutely distraught, but thanked the Angels for hearing my prayers, and I knew that she would be absolutely fine in her place of rest. After a while I realised I couldn't leave her body by the radiator so I picked her up gently and took her down the garden into my meditation room. I placed her on the carpet in the room and began to meditate.

What happened next startled me beyond belief. I heard a pattering on top of the summer house roof and then distinctly heard a cat mewing. My immediate thought was, "Oh my God, she isn't dead", and I leapt up from the chair and went over to her body – which was literally a shell now and of course it was completely still. I ran outside to see if there was another cat that had landed on the roof but there was nothing there. I truly believe that it was Topsy who had come to visit me one last time to let me know she was happy and pain-free.

I have felt her presence many times since she passed over, and I often feel her jumping on the bed even though I can't see her.

Four years later, our little dog Jet, who was now deaf and partially blind went off her legs and we had to rush her to the vets. A couple of evening before this happened I saw a misty image moving on the rug and realised it was my cat Topsy who passed over to the animal spirit world a few years ago. I felt that she was letting me know it was Jet's time and I mentioned this to my husband John. The day that she'd gone off her legs I rang the vet and they told me to bring her in straight away. Just before we were ready to leave, I went to switch the light on in the bathroom and the light bulb blew. I knew in that instance that we wouldn't be bringing Jet back home – it was spirit's way of preparing me for the inevitable and letting me know that her light in this world would be going out.

When we got to the vet it was an empty clinic; I feel the vet also knew that it was Jet's last day on Earth. We saw a lovely lady vet from America and she laid it on the line for us. Jet was extremely poorly. I had thought she was seventeen (she was a rescue dog) but they had her down as being twenty. All in all she was an old lady and in a lot of discomfort. Apparently she had a very infected womb and also had tumours in her body. The vet suspected cancer but couldn't be sure unless she operated, but even then they were not sure if Jet would pull through. We had a decision to make. Either we could put her through an operation that she may not survive, or we put her out of her misery and let her go without the discomfort of a serious operation. We decided on the latter.

We stayed with her throughout with me stroking her head. She knew I was there, but it was one of the hardest decisions I have ever made and both John and I were distraught. Back at home there was an empty hole and neither of us knew what to do with ourselves and of course there were constant reminders of Jet: her bed, her dish, toys, etc. But the guilt was the worst – had we made the right decision? I went to sit on the swing in the garden which was my favourite place and my white cat Celestial (Celeste for short) came straight away to sit on my knee and I felt she was comforting me. Libby came and rested her head on me and my other cat Tara was nearby. Animals know instinctively when someone isn't well and I feel they had known this about Jet for some time now. They were letting me know that I had done the right thing. I had expected Libby to be pining for Jet but she seemed happy and content.

Sitting in the conservatory comforting each other, I looked out of the window at the garden. Instantly I saw the image of Jet's head as clear as a bell as if it was suspended over the wisteria at the top of the trellis and I saw her as she was when she was younger, as if looking around. I turned to look behind me in case I had seen the reflection of my other dog Libby, although in my heart I knew I hadn't. Hearing Libby moving around upstairs proved it but of course when I looked back out of the window the vision had gone. However, I knew that without a doubt the angels had given me a vision of my lovely little dog to let me know she had made her final journey to the Rainbow Bridge. Isn't it wonderful to know that our pets, who are part of our family and a big part of our lives, can still visit us in the same way that our family or friends in spirit can?

Trooper

By Elizabeth Revill

Also by the author

The terrifying Inspector Allison psychological thrillers:

Killing me Softly
Prayer for the Dying
God only Knows
Would I Lie To You

Llewellyn Family Saga:

Whispers on the Wind
Shadows on the Moon
Rainbows in the Clouds
Thunder in the Sun

Stand alone novels:

Against the Tide
The Electra Conspiracy
Sanjukta and the Box of Souls
The Forsaken and the Damned

Trooper

By Elizabeth Revill

The scruffy grey and black fluffy mongrel scooted around the corner with his tail between his legs. He dodged another stone hurled at him by a young lad who laughed viciously as the pebble skimmed the animal's back, cutting into his fur and almost slicing through his skin to his backbone. The mutt yelped and ran harder in a desperate attempt to flee the bullying thug. He dived through some shrubbery and shivered miserably behind a blackcurrant bush.

Moonshine pooled on the path behind him like spilled milk. The opalescent sheen of light became mottled as wisps of travelling night clouds attempted to mask the baleful face of the moon.

The cruel boy with the spiked gelled hair ran past whooping in glee. Trooper followed the delinquent with his eyes, eyes that had more knowledge than a dog should. His head dropped and he hardly dared to move or breathe until he felt the danger had passed.

Trooper was a free spirit. Born into a loving family the dog knew he was different. He still did all the doggy things in the same way as his canine friends so as not to alert suspicion but he possessed knowledge and understanding, which surpassed that of other creatures.

After his family moved house he had been left behind. He knew they hadn't wanted to leave him and if he hadn't gone chasing after a saucy French Poodle who had waggled her butt at him he would have been safely stowed in the family car and followed the removal truck that had taken his home, bed and all his creature comforts to their new address.

He reprimanded himself as old habits die hard, to use a cliché. How did

Trooper know that? He couldn't explain it but somehow he did. It was strange, Trooper had the ability to think and reason and remember, but why?

His comfortable life was now all but a distant memory. Trooper had forgone his cosy loving home for the freedom and danger on the streets and although at first it had seemed exciting. He was now scared, tired of living on his wits and very hungry. He huddled quietly behind the bush and waited until he was sure the ruffian had moved on knowing the malevolent youth would be eager to torment some other stray or lost pet.

Trooper whimpered softly and lay down, his head on his paws, uncertain what to do or where to go next. He felt that there was a reason for his existence, a reason why he hadn't settled happily with his kind and adoptive family, a definite reason, and a reason he was destined to learn. His heart and mind told him that what would be would be. Words floated around his brain, 'everything happens for a reason.'

It was then he heard the music. He lifted his head and cocked it on one side. The lilting piano music was mournful but penetrated his soul. It awakened in him a need, a need for the warmth of loving human contact. But more than that it stirred in him a memory. Trooper knew that music and knew that delicate touch on the piano keys.

The young dog looked warily about him. The desire to search out the source of the music was strong. Should he leave the apparent safety of the bush and seek out the plaintive notes that called to him? Or should he use it as a diversion to escape the impoverished neighbourhood he had been trapped in? It was no good. Something stronger was calling him, something intangible, something inexplicable. The problem was Trooper's memories were not complete. It was if he was trying to grasp handfuls of fog to bottle and keep. There was always something missing.

Trooper hauled himself along on his tummy keeping low and crept along the path. His belly fur became more matted and encrusted with dirt as he scrawled along the ground, skirting over mud and puddles.

He whined softly in his throat. His little heart beat erratically but still he edged forward seeking to find the delicate harmonious piano symphony, which drifted on the night air. He knew when he found the source he would find his answers. There he would learn why he was able to think and reason as he did.

The little dog had reached the outskirts of the run down estate on the edge of town. There was a busy road to cross and beyond that was the safety of trees, countryside and that music.

He still heard the music in his head although Trooper knew that was impossible. The thunderous rumble of cars and lorries flashing through the night had all but drowned out the melancholy sound. Only when there was a lull in the monotonous drone of revving engines did the tune travel on the night breeze. His acute hearing picked up the sound easily.

Trooper stopped his stealthy crawl and stood up. He shook himself to remove the excess water and soil debris from his fur and scrambled under the wooden fence marking the boundary of the slum estate. Feeling more secure and confident he slid down the green embankment coming to a stop on the edge of the asphalt highway and waited.

His eyes alert as those of an owl prowling for prey watched and he paused. Vehicles roared past. No one took any notice of the little dog sitting patiently waiting to cross.

The route to the centre of the motorway although not far in terms of distance seemed almost out of reach such was the speed of the traffic as people raced to their destinations. Trooper waited. After a lorry and drag roared by eagerly followed by a convoy of smaller vehicles there was a suitable gap. Trooper ran to the central reservation and crouched down. His little heart was thumping so loudly it drowned out the bellowing traffic but still he could hear and feel the music in his soul.

Fleetingly he received an image of an attractive woman with burnished chestnut hair sitting at a piano lost in the plaintive tune she played. Her body swayed, her eyes were closed and Trooper was filled with great sadness.

Another truck rattled past disturbing his reverie. He watched the approaching cars. There were fewer vehicles running in this direction and it wasn't long before he could sprint to the other side.

His small pads skidded to a stop on the hard shoulder and he clambered up the bank. For some reason he was consumed with nervous apprehension. His stomach twisted into wringing knots and he tried to quell the seemingly irrational grip of fear.

Trooper burrowed under the chain link fence and stepped into the trees that graced the edge of the land. He was surefooted in his loping stride and he ran spurred on by something that was calling him.

A nightjar shrieked on its nocturnal hunt as it foraged for food. Trooper's ears lifted up; pricked to attention to capture and savour all he could hear. He ran on through the woods, across a stream, passing small roe deer exploring the space and nibbling the soft new shoots that sprouted from young saplings.

On and on he travelled. "It's like the Incredible Journey," thought Trooper and then stopped suddenly. What was the incredible journey? How did he know about it? Why had he thought about it? Trooper shook his coat, sat and listened, his head on one side, trying to capture the direction of the melody, which he could hear more clearly and was becoming stronger.

Other sounds filtered through into his consciousness, which spurred him to take cover. He disappeared inside a hollow tree trunk and waited. Two men crashed past through the undergrowth. Twigs cracked and snapped. He caught a fleeting glimpse of a burly, stocky man in a thick padded jacket with a rifle slung over his shoulder. His companion was a scrawny youth with acne pitted skin and patchy whiskers as if he was too young to grow a beard. They emitted a sour acrid smell. Trooper almost whimpered in fear but knew he dared not make a sound. The smaller man carried a large canvas bag and the older man wore a ski mask that obliterated his broad features and he carried a brace of rabbits.

The men moved on in the direction of a country village where few lights could be seen. Most people were safely asleep in their beds but one or two properties with lights blazing indicated the occupants were awake.

Trooper crept out of hiding and followed. The men marched through the field toward the first farmhouse where they appeared to bid each other goodbye. The gangling youth took the rabbits and hurried toward a small outbuilding on the adjacent farmland. The bigger man put his masked face up to the leprous moon, which reflected in the light of man's eyes.

Trooper shuddered. He didn't like what he saw. The eyes revealed an alien presence of one that had resided with demons in hell. The man's head snapped around to the sound of the music and stepped out with renewed vigour to the isolated cottage close to the village church. The dog followed cautiously, careful to remain hidden and like a sniper on a mercenary mission held back just enough not to attract any attention.

A gravel path led to the front door of the lonely farmhouse. The man's boots crunched loudly on the small stones. He stepped off onto the soft grass to mask his approach and ventured like a fugitive toward the window where a piano played.

The poacher ducked down out of sight and peered in through the softly lit window. The drapes were open and shielded the woman's view of the night, whilst marauding intruders were able to watch at their leisure.

The man divested himself of his coat and laid it out on the grass, next to his rifle. Underneath he wore a ripped, tatty tee shirt that had faded proclaiming the slogan, 'Life or Death. You choose.'

Trooper watched.

The man continued to peer into the room. His hand drifted to his groin and he began to rub himself through his heavy denim jeans. As if that wasn't and wouldn't be enough he stopped, picked up his firearm and tiptoed around the house out of sight.

Trooper whined gently in his throat. He trotted to the window and looked in on the scene. A small growl erupted in his throat as he recognised the woman and he tried to suppress the soft mewling that threatened to burst from him. Trooper's gaze fixed on the woman. His eyes filled with unconditional love and he knew he had to get inside.

There was a splintering crunch as the thickset man burst in through the door and broke into the music room. The woman stopped playing and her hand flew up to her throat in horror as the man was upon her. He ripped her from the piano stool and flung her onto the sheepskin rug where she lay paralysed with fear.

She looked too terrified to scream although she attempted to cry out but no sound would come. The beast straddled her struggling crazily with his trouser zip. He pinned her down quite easily.

She was slim and small in stature almost ethereal looking with her cloud of chestnut tresses, dressed in a white transparent robe, which revealed her body's curvaceous silhouette.

Trooper growled more angrily now, he drew his lips back in anger revealing his wolfish teeth. His hackles rose and he knew he had to do something.

The dog ran back from the window and loped forward, taking a giant leap into the air. Without thinking the little dog hurled himself at the glass pane, which shattered with such ferocity that glass shards exploded onto the floor and rained down onto the man's back.

Trooper jumped onto the brute's shoulders and sunk his teeth into the man's neck growling like a ravaged bear. The man flailed his arms attempting to fling the animal off but Trooper clung to him like a terrier would savage a rat. He would not let go. His grip was so tight that blood began to flow from the man's neck and down his chest.

The young woman crawled away from the brutal assault and took cover under the piano. Her face was constricted with fear. She watched as the man rose up and danced in agony trying to shake off the young dog. As if coming to her senses, she emerged from hiding and grabbed the rifle firing a shot into the ceiling.

The man's eyes now filled with fear and loathing as he stumbled toward her but still Trooper held on tightly. He twisted and turned, this way and that as the young woman now woken from her stupor rushed to the phone and dialled nine, nine, nine.

Her voice was clear and resolute in spite of a slight tremor. "Police please. I'm being attacked. A man has broken into my house and has tried to rape me. My dog is keeping him at bay. The Granary... Yes... Next door to the church. Please hurry." She replaced the phone keeping the gun trained on him.

The beast managed to grasp the animal and tear him off his back. He flung Trooper at the woman and fled, leaving his rifle in her hands. The dog's teeth had slashed his throat and he was bleeding profusely. He was lucky that his artery had not been severed.

The man blundered out and made his escape. Trooper looked up into the face of the woman that he knew so well and whined softly at her. She lay down the gun and stooped to ruffle his fur. He licked her hand gently and rolled over. The woman sat down on the settee and called the mongrel to her. "You saved my life. If it hadn't been for you... " She stopped and choked back a sob, "If you don't have a home. You have one now with me."

She patted the seat next to her and Trooper jumped up and snuggled into her. Sirens could be heard approaching as a police car made its way through the village to the converted barn known as the Granary.

Trooper gazed around the familiar room, the plaster cast whorls, the splashes of aubergine that lifted the magnolia of the walls, the heavy dark beams and lovingly chosen furniture. His eyes caught the picture framed on the table of his beloved Alice in happier times with him. He jumped off the sofa and trotted to the piano and barked at the picture. She crossed to him and picked up the photograph and returned to her seat.

Trooper followed.

She smoothed down his fur and as if feeling a need, a compunction to talk, the words flooded from her.

"That's me, five years ago." Trooper barked and whined putting a paw out to try and swipe at the picture. "And that was my husband, Jake. I loved him desperately but he was killed in a road accident. So sad." She paused as she remembered, "Things were just getting back on track. We were rediscovering the joy of each other after all that pain. He'd had an affair, you see, with another teacher at school. He taught English. She taught French. He regretted it. I know he did. It was senseless, meaningless and damaging but we would have got through it. It would have made us stronger..." Alice sighed and a tear escaped her eyes as the sirens grew louder and police lights reflected around the room.

Two coppers entered and noted the disarray, broken glass and mess. Alice handed them the rifle, which one of them recognised. They exchanged a glance before sitting down and Alice began her statement. She concluded, "If Trooper here hadn't come to my aid... I shudder to think what would have happened..."

The dog looked up at the sound of his name and Alice whispered, "I'm calling you Trooper. We always said when we got a dog that's what we'd call him. I know Jake would be pleased."

The police finished taking notes and called for someone to come and board up the window until a replacement could be fitted. One of them radioed ahead to call for a warrant to arrest Colin Beer. After checking that she would be all right they left Alice and Trooper together and drove off into the night.

Alice looked deep into Trooper's eyes. "You have an old soul," she pronounced. "I can see it... in fact you have eyes like Jake. He had those spaniel eyes that were so expressive... just like you."

Trooper licked her hand again and snuggled up to her. He was home, where he belonged and although not quite as he wanted to be. It would be enough.

Lightning Source UK Ltd.
Milton Keynes UK
UKOW04f1831271015

261485UK00001B/152/P